PUFFIN

SUPER GRAN

She's on the warpath again: Super Gran, the Super senior citizen with X-ray eyes and unbelievable strength! And it's her most difficult assignment yet, because the devilish Inventor has got his hands on an invincible shield. Nothing can penetrate it: knives, bullets, even death-rays! Only Super Gran can stop the Inventor from conquering the world. But will even her powers be strong enough?

This is Forrest Wilson's third book featuring the marvellously comic little lady with Super powers. Read about her other adventures in the enormously popular *Super Gran, Super Gran Rules O K!* and *Super Gran is Magic,* all published in Puffin.

Forrest Wilson

SUPER GRAN SUPERSTAR

Illustrated by David McKee

Puffin Books

To the members
of the Puffin Book Club

Puffin Books, Penguin Books Ltd, Harmondsworth, Middlesex, England
Penguin Books, 40 West 23rd Street, New York, New York 10010, U.S.A.
Penguin Books Australia Ltd, Ringwood, Victoria, Australia
Penguin Books Canada Ltd, 2801 John Street, Markham, Ontario, Canada L3R 1B4
Penguin Books (N.Z.) Ltd, 182–190 Wairau Road, Auckland 10, New Zealand

First published 1982
Reprinted 1982, 1983

Made and printed in Great Britain by
Cox & Wyman Ltd, Reading
Set in Monophoto Baskerville by
Northumberland Press Ltd,
Gateshead, Tyne and Wear

Contents

1 Meals on Wheels

Edison Faraday Black emerged from the supermarket to join her father, who had been waiting for her outside in his wheelchair.

'Look!' Mr Black exclaimed, pointing.

In the distance, but rapidly approaching them, careering down the High Street at full speed on a rusted, discarded skateboard, came a little old lady. She was dressed for the part in a bashed, tattered crash helmet and torn second-hand knee and elbow pads and she zigzagged in and out of the traffic.

She weaved her way across occupied zebra crossings, scattering cross crossers in every direction. She clanked on and off pavements and narrowly avoided the crowds of shoppers, mothers with prams, patrolling traffic wardens, policemen on point duty, buses, lorries, cars and cyclists. And in her hands she held a large stack of covered tin plates, balanced precariously one on top of the other, leaning like a tottering Tower of Pisa!

It was Super Gran!

As she approached Edison and Mr Black she whistled. And the girl and her father – and everyone else within earshot! – shot their fingers into their ears to prevent themselves being Super-deafened!

'Hello, Super Gran ...' Edison waved to her old

friend – who promptly waved back at her! 'No, Super Gran – don't wave! Your hands are full . . . !'

The girl closed her eyes, shuddered to think what would happen and waited to hear the expected crash of the tin-plated meals all over the street.

But, by some miracle, the crash never came. Somehow, with a nifty piece of Super-juggling, Super Gran managed to keep not only her *own* balance but also the balance of the teetering pile of plates, as she swept on down the High Street, scything a path through pedestrians, who hurriedly jumped out of her way, and traffic, which hastily braked to let her past.

'Is that her version of "Meals on Wheels"?' Edison's father asked, as Super Gran disappeared into the distance.

'Yes, *one* of them!' Edison laughed, as she pushed her father in his chair along the street.

Delivering Meals on Wheels was Super Gran's way of helping the town's old people, after feeling guilty about playing with her Super-powers instead of doing some good with them.

'But I thought she'd roped in Tub, Mrs Preston and the other Super-Oldies to help with Meals on Wheels?' Mr Black went on.

'She did. They *do* help. But they do it the *proper* way, delivering the dinners in the normal Meals on Wheels vans. It's just that Super Gran has her own way of doing things.'

'You're not joking!' her father muttered.

In the short time that Super Gran had been involved

in the Meals on Wheels service she had contrived to find every, and any, way of interpreting the phrase. She had delivered the meals on almost every type of wheel you could possibly imagine!

To begin with she had used Willard's bicycle, on which she had whizzed round the town, narrowly missing collisions with everyone who got in her way. She rang the bicycle bell at them, of course, but if they didn't dodge her quickly enough she whistled at them.

Super Gran had never whistled before in her life. When she was young it was considered unladylike to whistle. But now that she was old she didn't care about being unladylike! And she had discovered that not only could she whistle, she could Super-whistle. Which made everyone who came near her jump – almost out of their skins! Especially those she whistled at from close quarters!

'Tch!' she'd scolded herself. 'I keep forgetting how Super my Super-powers are!'

However, Willard's bike didn't last long. For Super Gran was too Super-rough with it – and it fell to pieces! And while she waited for it to be repaired – and made Super-Gran proof! – she had tried all sorts of different wheels. From Edison's roller-disco skates and an old battered pram which she found on a dump to Tub's brand-new motor-bike (which she didn't have a licence to drive!).

And on one occasion she had even used an electric-cable drum no longer in use. Balanced precariously on top of it, she had 'walked' it along the road at speed,

9

like a circus performer, and had exclaimed loudly to everyone she passed: 'Look folks – Meals on *Reels*!'

'It's a wonder,' Mr Black commented, 'that she doesn't use the *Skimmer* for her Meals on Wheels. That would be ideal, wouldn't it?' He was referring to the invention which Super Gran and company had recently tried out in London.

'*Would* have been, you mean!' Edison corrected, as they turned down a side street, heading towards the public park.

'What do you mean "would have been"? And that reminds me, what *happened* to the Skimmer? None of you mentioned it and I've been too busy to ask. You told me about your adventures and Super Gran's reward for recovering the Arab Crown Jewels. But you didn't say a word about the Skimmer.'

Edison, pushing the wheelchair in through the park gates, explained: 'Super Gran was so busy catching Roly Poley and his gang at the Tower, and jumping across Tower Bridge,' – Edison shuddered at the thought – 'that she forgot to remove the anti-theft device key – and somebody stole the Skimmer!'

Mr Black laughed.

'I don't know what *you're* laughing at,' Edison retorted. 'You'll have to build another one now. For the government. 'Cos they wanted it!'

'Oh, don't worry, I'll just send 'em the plans, drawings and details,' he replied airily, with a dismissive wave. '*I'm* not building them another one. I'm too busy working on a *new* invention.'

'Humph! You always *are*. I just hope it's another Super-machine, to make the rest of Super Gran's friends super, like herself.'

'She's not *still* going on about that, is she?' Mr Black asked, as they moved along the park's main pathway.

'She sure is,' Edison assured him.

'Well you can tell the old nag I've got other plans. And my new invention's something even better than the Super-mach –'

'Tell her yourself,' Edison interrupted, pointing. 'Here she comes now . . .'

Super Gran, having completed her Meals on Wheels rounds, but still on her skateboard, had entered the park through a side entrance and was zooming towards the football pitches in front of Edison, where some boys were already playing. She had arranged to meet Willard, her grandson, who was forever going on about having a proper, full-length, uninterrupted game of football with her – for once! For he and his pals *never* seemed to finish their games with Super Gran.

Just then, approaching Edison and her father from another direction, came a newspaper reporter. Or at least, that's what he *said* he was.

'Excuse me,' he greeted them politely, 'do you know where I can find Super Gran? I'm told she likes playing football and . . .'

'Yes,' Edison interrupted, pointing. 'That's her over there with those boys.'

Edison thought that there was something familiar

about the man, although she wasn't sure where she had seen him before.

He was bald-headed and had a greying beard and thick, black, bushy eyebrows. And it seemed to be the thick, black, bushy eyebrows which Edison recognized!

The Inventor, in his house bordering the park, was still determined to rule the world and wasn't going to be put off by a little set-back like Super Gran and a dozen Super-Oldies. Not that this had been his opinion immediately after his battle in the park with them, but he had regained his courage and his confidence by now.

He had paced up and down his wasted workshop (wrecked by Super Gran's friend, Mrs Preston, after she had been made Super) for weeks on end, racking his crooked brains to think of a way to make a comeback – but without success.

Then recently, while Benny his bad buddy had been visiting him, an idea had struck the Inventor. Or rather, something which Benny said, in his usual slow way, triggered it off in the Inventor's mind.

'Yus, there ... we were ... like,' Benny was saying, as he relived the excitement of a game of snooker which he and his 'boys' – the Toughies – had had, the previous evening. 'I had to ... pot the ... black before ... the boys ... potted the ... black, like ... and ...'

'That's it! That's it!' The Inventor jumped out of his chair excitedly – and then gasped with pain. Benny had been demonstrating his snooker stroke at the time and his fist had accidentally connected with the Inventor's jaw!

Einstein, the Inventor's cat, looked up at the men for a moment from where he lay beside the fireplace, and then went back to sleep again. If these men wanted to assault each other it was no concern of his!

'Ouch!' The Inventor rubbed his jaw tenderly. 'Yes, that's it. Black ...'

'Yeah, Professor ... it was ... the black. I was ... just about ... to stun it ... into the ... pocket, an' ...'

'No, no, I didn't mean black – I meant *Black* ...'

'Yeah, black ...' Benny repeated.

'No, *Black* ...!' the Inventor insisted. 'Not "black", a snooker ball. "Black", the inventor ...'

Yes, that was it, he thought. It was easy, now that he thought of it. But why hadn't he thought of it sooner? It was the answer to all his problems. He could kick himself for wasting all that time. To think that he could have been well on his way to ruling the world by now, if only he had thought of it sooner.

While Benny continued with his story of how he and Gruff had snookered Rough and Tough, the Inventor was rabbiting on about how Benny and his Toughies could help him become world-ruler. So neither man heard what the other was muttering about for the next half-hour!

Eventually, when he had worked out his plans, the Inventor told Benny to belt up and listen to him. Or, to be more precise (because the Inventor was scared stiff of Benny and his boys – and with good reason!),

13

he waited until Benny stopped for a breath, and then he spoke!

'Benny, I want you and the Toughies ... er, that is ... your boys, to do a job for me.'

'Sure, boss ... anythin' ... what is it ... like ... ?'

'I want you to kidnap Black for me, and ...'

'Kidnap?' Benny muttered, looking puzzled. 'Kidnap a ... black snooker ... ball, like ... ?'

'No! Don't be daft, Benny ... er, that is ... I mean ... no Benny, *not* a black snooker ball. Black, the inventor. *Mister* Black.'

Benny grinned. 'Yeah, me too! I mister black ... last night ... at snooker ... !' He guffawed. He had made a joke!

The Inventor's plan – like Benny – was simple! Benny and his boys would kidnap Edison's father and make him build another Super-machine – for the Inventor. In fact, nothing could be simpler. They had previously stolen the original Super-machine from Mr Black, so all they had to do now was steal Mr Black himself!

'You can do it tonight if you like, when it's dark.'

But Benny shook his head, slowly, after he had thought it out, slowly! 'No boss ... tonight's no ... good, like. I've gotta ... date at a ... bank, tonight ... after midnight ...'

'But the banks don't open after midnight, Benny. They close at ...' The puzzled Inventor suddenly realized what Benny meant. 'Oh, I see ... !' For Benny didn't intend entering the bank the normal, legal way!

'On the other hand,' the Inventor continued thoughtfully, 'maybe I'd better arrange to get Super Gran out of the way first. Before you kidnap Black. M'mm, now let's think about this . . .'

Presently the Inventor worked out a plan. 'Benny, will you and your boys be available next Saturday afternoon? Or Sunday?'

'Well, let's . . . see now . . .' Benny racked his brains. 'We're all . . . busy on . . . Sat'day an' . . . *I've* gotta . . . job Sunday . . . afternoon. But . . . the boys'll . . . be free, like . . .'

'Right. Sunday afternoon it is. Super Gran likes to play football, I believe, so we'll fix her up with a game, shall we? A *special* game!' He cackled and rubbed his hands together in eager anticipation.

A friend of his ran an amateur football team and he knew that the man would be willing, for a few pounds, to lend out a couple of teams for a match. And he also knew that Benny could supply him with a few more 'toughies', to order. (Sort of 'Renta Ruffians'!) So he outlined his plan to Benny.

The Inventor would be world-ruler in no time at all. Just as soon as he had Mr Black in his clutches, to build him a new Super-machine. 'You see, Benny, it's my destiny to be world-ruler,' he murmured, 'my destiny . . .'

'Eh?' Benny looked down at the Inventor's trouser-leg, mystified. 'Your . . . dusty knee . . . ?'

'No, not my dusty knee, my destiny . . . Oh, never mind! Can your boys fetch their van along on Sunday afternoon? To carry Black *and* his wheelchair?'

'We don't ... 'ave a van ... but we'll ... *get* one ...'
Benny said. 'Out a ... car park ...'

'You mean, steal one?'

'Yeah! We just ... pick 'em ... an' nick 'em ... !'
Benny rhymed and laughed. He was a poet!

2   A Match for Super Gran?

'So you're a bit of a footballer, Super Gran?' the reporter said, after he had introduced himself to the old lady. And after he had persuaded her to stop playing football long enough to listen to him!

'She sure is.' Willard, dribbling the ball from foot to foot, chipped in before his Gran could reply. He remembered how she had out-manoeuvred him and his pals as she played with them soon after she had first become Super. It was a pity, he thought, that she didn't play with them more often, but she always seemed to have other things to do. 'And *I'm* good too!' he added proudly. Willard had no modesty where football was concerned!

'Oh ... ah ... are you, sonny?' The man ignored Willard and turned to Super Gran to explain: 'It's a special match. For charity. Against a local amateur team, Spinkton Spurs.'

'Oh aye?' Super Gran wasn't impressed. It was hardly Liverpool or Manchester United!

'We'd like you to play in this match with them,' the reporter continued. 'We'll have photographers there and it's in aid of ... ah ... um ... a poor old man who ... ah ... wants to be world-rul – er, that is ... who wants to get on in the world! And he's just about down to his last fiver ...'

'Aw, is that so? Poor old soul,' Super Gran sympathized.

'So you'll play?' The man's eyes lit up like the Blackpool illuminations.

'M'mm, I don't know, laddie ...' She wasn't wholly convinced.

'Go on, Gran. It'll be a great game,' Willard coaxed her.

'I don't know,' Super Gran repeated. 'Let's see now – Spinkton's ten miles away, isn't it? How will we get there?'

'We could borrow some bikes,' Willard suggested eagerly.

'Yes,' the reporter quickly agreed, 'and the children would certainly enjoy watching you play football, Super Gran, and ...'

'Watchin'?' Willard exploded. 'Watchin'? *I'm* not goin' to be watchin'. *I'm* goin' to be playin'!'

'But you're too young, sonny,' the man frowned, 'you might get hurt. It's *men* you'd be playing against, not little boys.'

'*I* don't mind.' Willard glowered at him. 'I'll play football against *any*body! I'm not scared!'

'Well, I dunno ...' The reporter, uncertain, was thinking it over.

'Look, laddie,' Super Gran addressed the man grimly. (She called everyone 'laddie', whatever their age!) 'If wee Willard here's not playing, then *I'm* not playing! See?'

'But he's *too* wee ... er ... I mean, he's too small,' the reporter protested.

'But *I'm* wee too,' Super Gran pointed out. 'I'm just a poor, wee, defenceless little old lady.'

Edison, Willard and Mr Black burst out laughing at this. If there was anything that Super Gran was *not*, it was a defenceless little old lady!

'Okay, okay,' the man gave in. 'The boy can play too.'

Willard grinned happily.

'And the girl will come, to spectate?' the man went on anxiously.

'I wouldn't miss it,' Edison replied eagerly.

The reporter gave a sigh of relief. He'd had to make sure that all three of them would be there. And he had got the dithering Super Gran to stop dithering when she thought that Willard wasn't going to be allowed to play. It had all been part of the plan.

He turned to walk away. 'See you on Sunday afternoon then? Spinkton recreation grounds. Two o'clock. Right?'

'You realize,' Super Gran called after him, 'that I've only played football with two or three wee laddies before? Never with real grown-up men.'

'Oh ... ah ... is that so?' The reporter hesitated, frowning.

'Aw, don't worry, Gran,' Willard assured her. 'You'll be great. You'll be super. You can't *help* bein' Super!' he laughed. 'And with me on your side you'll be even Super-er!'

'They'll give you a good game,' the reporter said, as he turned to walk away across the grass. But they didn't hear what he added under his breath: 'A good *hard*, *rough*, *tough* game!'

He cackled happily as he walked towards the park's exit.

So everything was settled. Super Gran and the children would cycle to Spinkton on the Sunday and Willard and his Gran, with nine other players from another team would face the Spinkton Spurs. And Press photographers would be there, so Super Gran should get plenty of publicity from the write-up and the pictures which would appear in the local paper.

However, if Super Gran had tuned in her Super-hearing to a conversation which was taking place in a rusty old 'banger' parked outside the park gates, she would have had second thoughts about the whole thing.

For the 'reporter', who had stripped off his 'bald-headed' wig and his false beard as he climbed in beside Benny, was giving an account of his Oscar-worthy performance in the park.

'Dis guy's in disguise!' he guffawed, adding: 'She fell for it. They all did, the idiots!'

Benny put the car into gear and it roared away from the kerb, spluttering and protesting.

'I told her it was for charity,' the Inventor laughed, 'and so it is. But charity begins at home, doesn't it? I told them it was for a poor old man, down to his last fiver. And that's what *I* am. But not for long, eh? Not for long.'

He rubbed his hands together greedily, as he and

Benny roared with laughter. Once he was world-ruler, he would be rich . . .

The car suddenly spluttered to a halt. It was out of petrol! Benny clambered wearily out, to walk to the nearest filling station to buy a canful.

The Inventor produced the last bank-note from his wallet. 'I said I was down to my last fiver, didn't I?'

On Sunday afternoon Super Gran and the children cycled the ten miles to Spinkton on borrowed bikes, Super Gran arriving there Super-fresh, Willard arriving a bit out of breath and Edison, as usual, arriving puffing, panting and completely breathless. For Edison was anything but athletic.

They thought they would never make it in time for the kick-off, as Edison had to stop every quarter of a mile or so for a rest and to get her breath back. But after a couple of miles Super Gran decided to cycle behind Edison – and push her the rest of the way!

Once there, Willard joined the other players in the little wooden hut which served as the dressing-room. He stripped off his outdoor clothes and put on his football strip and boots. Super Gran, who didn't believe in dressing for the occasion and was just going to play in her ordinary clothes – a floral dress, cardigan and tartan tammy – waited outside for Willard and the others to get ready.

Before the game started Edison, who was standing at the side touchline near their discarded bicycles, noticed that there was no sign of the 'reporter'.

'Yeah, and where are the photographers?' asked a disappointed Willard, when he and his Gran had rejoined her. He was eager to see a football action-photo of himself in the newspapers, and perhaps to be 'discovered' by some big, important First Division team.

Super Gran looked around at the eight spectators who were patiently waiting for the match to start. 'Aye, and another thing – if this game's for charity, they won't make much out of this wee crowd. And it doesn't look as if they paid to come in, either!'

'No, it's only an ordinary playing field,' Edison agreed. 'There aren't any pay-boxes or turnstiles or anything.'

'Yeah, and there are more players in one *team*,' Willard pointed out, 'than there are watchin' the game!'

'Aye, I'm beginning to think there's maybe something funny going on here,' Super Gran admitted, as the players emerged from the dressing-room on to the playing field and were joined by the referee, who started the game.

And what a game it was!

When Super Gran got the ball passed to her, and before she could do anything with it, she found no less than *six* of the opposing players appearing from nowhere, it seemed, and charging straight towards her! She side-stepped the first one, but another two of them shoulder-charged her – one to each shoulder! – and sandwiched her roughly in between them.

'Ouch, you scunners!' she cried, as they crushed her.

Then the other four opponents crowded in and

23

obstructed her, even though she no longer had possession of the ball.

The referee blew his whistle for a foul, which Willard quickly took. But again, when he passed the ball to his Gran he saw that she was being surrounded by the same six players whose sole objective, it seemed, was to crowd Super Gran out of the game. They made no attempt whatsoever to go near the ball, Willard saw, and he wondered what their idea was. Playing football actually seemed to be the *last* thing that they wanted to do! In fact, he wondered if they *could* play football – it didn't *look* as if they could!

And Super Gran was beginning to think that she had six shadows! They just wouldn't leave her alone for a moment. Not for a second! Everywhere *she* went, *they* went! If *she* ran, *they* ran. If *she* strolled, *they* strolled. If *she* stood still, *they* stood still. It's one thing to mark your man – but this was ridiculous! And it was all very well for Super Gran to be Super, but up against six hefty he-men who wouldn't give her an inch of room – she just didn't stand a chance.

Meanwhile, the game continued with Willard and his nine team-mates against the five opponents who *weren't* busy marking Super Gran and, naturally, it didn't take long for Willard's side to score.

'What's going on, laddie?' she whispered to him breathlessly, as they walked to the centre of the park for the after-goal kick-off. 'What are those haggis-heads up to?'

'Dunno!' Willard shrugged. 'Why don't you try . . . ?'

He was going to suggest her 'mind-reading', but before he could say it Super Gran was zooming down the pitch again. She gained possession of the ball and tried to dribble it away from her six bodyguards.

But once again she was unsuccessful. Neither her Super-strength nor her Super-speed was a match for the six large, rugged ruffians. For they descended on her as one man and they pushed, pulled, shoved, tugged and crowded her off the ball, which she lost to the other fifteen players who were actually playing normal football!

Again Super Gran's team scored – without her help! And again, at the kick-off, she tried to talk to Willard about them. But this time her six faithful followers stood on the centre-line, as near to her as possible, and before she could utter a word the referee's whistle blew, the ball was centred – and the suffocating six smothered her once more!

And this time they practically trampled her underfoot!

'Hey! Help! What's ... going ... on?' she mumbled, from the bottom of a heap of seven bodies, which resembled a *rugby scrum* rather than a *soccer tackle*! 'Jings! What's ... the big ... idea ... you big ... bachles?' she gasped breathlessly. 'I've heard of ... the "Dirty Dozen". But you lot ... are the ..."Dirty Half-Dozen"!'

She eventually managed to pull herself from the mass – but only after she had lashed out with feet and fists at the bodies all around her. She staggered to her feet, feeling as if she had just lost World War Three! Except that no one had told her that war had been declared!

She just had time to straighten her tammy, re-button her cardigan and take a deep breath before the 'Dirty Half-Dozen' descended on her once again. But luckily this time the referee saw what was happening and blew for a foul. One of the players took the kick and passed the ball to Willard, who dribbled it past two defenders and scored.

Instead of walking back for the kick-off, Super Gran ran to the touchline, where Edison stood near the eight spectators.

'What do *you* think they're playing at, lassie?'

'Well, it's not football, that's for sure!' Edison replied grimly.

'Jings! They remind me of that scunnersome Inventor's "Toughies" – twice over!' Super Gran said breathlessly.

'Toughies?' Edison snapped her fingers. 'That's it!'

'What's it?'

'I *thought* there was something familiar about that reporter,' Edison said. 'It was his bushy black eye-brows!'

'You mean . . . ?'

'The Inventor!' Edison gasped. 'He's behind all this!'

3   Footballers – Balled Out!

'So *that's* it? *He* arranged this match?' Super Gran exclaimed. 'But why?'

'To get those big bullies to bully you?' Edison suggested. 'To get his own back on you for beating him and his gang that time with the Super-machine?'

Super Gran shook her head. 'No, it's a lot of bother to go to just for that. There must be another reason.'

'Why don't you read their minds?' Edison said, being more successful than Willard had been with the suggestion.

'Aye, good idea, lassie. I'll do that.'

Meanwhile the game had re-started and was progressing without Super Gran. But as she had never been in it from the start that didn't really matter much! And besides, she now had more important things to do.

She turned her attention to each of her six shadows (who stood around looking lost, watching her but not knowing what to do about her!), and she read their minds. Not that there was much to read, so it didn't take long!

'Ah-ha!' she said triumphantly, seconds later. 'You were right, lassie. It *was* the Inventor who put them up to it. I can see a picture of him in their minds.'

She rolled up her 'cardi' sleeves, ready for battle. 'Right, that does it!'

'What're you going to do, Super Gran?'

'I don't know, but I'll think of something!'

Super Gran spotted the groundsman's shed behind the dressing-room. She ran over to it, opened the small side door and disappeared inside. Two of the tough guys ran after her.

Edison was worried. Especially when she saw another two of the rented ruffians pointing to the shed and their pursuing mates, who, like Super Gran, had disappeared inside.

Suddenly there was an outburst of thuds and yells from the shed – then a deadly silence! Followed by more thumps and shouts as the second pair of toughies arrived, followed by even more bangs and howls after the third set ran to the shed and, like everyone else, disappeared inside.

Edison, *really* worried now, didn't know what to do. The football match was still in progress and she wondered if she should stop it and get Willard and the others to go and rescue Super Gran.

But there was no need. Edison should have known better! As if Super Gran needed *anyone*'s help!

The shed's large front double doors opened slightly as Super Gran popped her head out, pushed the doors fully open and then disappeared inside again. Then the peace and quiet was shattered by a roaring, spluttering noise as the groundsman's tractor and trailer emerged, with the old lady perched precariously at the controls!

The football match was forgotten as the players stopped to watch the erratically driven tractor zigzagging its way from the shed to the playing field. While on the trailer there was a heap of struggling, wriggling bodies which was in fact two sets of tough guys (with three in each set) – roped together!

The tractor reached the goalpost, where Super Gran switched off the engine and jumped down. Then she reached up, grabbed one set of fake footballers, hauled them from the trailer and tied them to one of the goalposts! Then she did the same with the other set of three, tying them to the other goalpost.

Grimly and silently, but with a wicked glint in her eye, Super Gran picked up the discarded football and placed it on the penalty spot. Then she ran up and kicked the ball, but not at the goal – at the goalpost!

'Ouch!' yelled one of the hoodlums as the ball, Super-kicked by Super Gran, contacted with a thud, knocking the breath from him.

'It's penalty-kick time – and this is the "penalty" you pay for trying to bully Super Gran!' she stormed.

She then replaced the ball on the spot and did the same thing again; and again, until she had 'scored' six times in all, against each of the six bullies in turn, to a chorus of 'Ow! Ouch! Ooyah! Stop it!' and 'Help, mother!' from the tough guys, who were now feeling more tender than tough!

Then, dusting off her hands, she walked away. 'Fetch your clothes, laddie,' she instructed Willard, as she signalled for him and Edison to pick up their bicycles,

leaving behind them fourteen footballers, all eager to use the bully boys as target practice!

'Wow! What was all *that* about, Gran?' Willard asked, as they cycled out of the recreation ground into the main road, heading for home. 'And what're we rushin' for?'

'We're *not* Russian, we're British!' Edison joked, but she was already too far behind the others for them to hear her!

Super Gran hadn't given Willard, who was still clutching his outdoor clothes, time to change out of his football gear. *And*, as usual, he didn't get to finish his match with her! He was fated!

'*Did* you read their minds, Super Gran?' Edison shouted towards the others, as she tried to catch up with them. 'What did you find?'

'I was supposed to get mad at those six scunnery-heads,' Super Gran shouted back to Edison, 'and spend all afternoon fighting them. And I'd be busy doing that while that wee pest the Inventor went about his crooked business!'

'The Inventor?' Willard gasped. 'What's *he* got to do with it?'

'He's just about to kidnap Edison's Dad, that's all!'

'Oh no!' the girl cried, as the others slowed down a bit to let her catch up with them.

'Oh aye!' Super Gran replied grimly.

'What'll we do?'

'What else? Get home as quick as we can and stop 'em! Come on! Hurry up! What's keeping you?'

'Hey! Wait for me!' Edison cried, as Willard pedalled off fast and Super Gran pedalled off – even faster!

'I'll go on ahead,' the old lady called back to the children. 'You come along at your own speed. I'll see you later, at Edison's house ...' And she zoomed off down the road to Chisleton, leaving behind her Willard cycling as fast as he could and Edison breathlessly taking her first rest – having cycled about a quarter of a mile!

Meanwhile the Inventor, thinking that he had at least two hours in which to snatch his victim, was organizing Benny's boys, in Benny's absence.

The Inventor, naturally, wasn't going to get involved in the actual kidnapping. He was merely going to instruct the Toughies (Rough, Tough and Gruff, as *he* called them) in what *they* had to do. After all, what if something went wrong and *he* were caught? *He* wasn't a criminal, he reckoned – *they* were! Let *them* take the risk!

'This is my chance,' he explained, 'to get hold of that confounded Black, and ...'

'That confounded black wot?' Rough asked, roughly – which was the way he always spoke. And which was why the Inventor had called him 'Rough' in the first place. (Apart, of course, from the fact that he *was* rough!)

'*Mister* Black!' the Inventor sighed. 'The man who invented the Super-machine. The man you pinched it from, remember?'

'OH? THAT MR BLACK?' shouted Tough, the smallest but loudest Toughie, who spoke only in shouts.

The Inventor reeled back, his hands covering his assaulted ears, deafened by the blast! 'Yes. Him,' he whispered.

'Wot d'we want this Black geezer for, boss?' Rough rasped, as he practised one of his feats of strength, infuriating the Inventor. (He was tying the Inventor's favourite fireside poker into half a dozen knots!)

'Wot ... er, that is ... *what* we want him for,' the Inventor explained, glaring from the knotty poker to the naughty Rough, 'is to make us another Super-machine. One that *I* can use and which that nuisance Super Gran won't get her tiny, little-old-lady's hands on.'

'DO WE BRING 'IM 'ERE?' yelled Tough, sending the Inventor staggering back again, his ears ringing.

'No, take him to Benny's place.' The Inventor shook his head, to clear it. 'They'll never think of looking for him there.'

'Right, boss,' Rough grated.

'SURE THING,' Tough roared.

'Ugh!' Gruff muttered, which was all that the Inventor had *ever* heard Gruff mutter.

'When d'we leave?' Rough asked, as he threw the poker into the fireplace, smashing three tiles in the process! Not to mention scaring the wits out of Einstein the cat, who had been dozing peacefully on the fireside rug!

'Now,' the Inventor told him, wincing at the damage

done to the fireplace. And the sooner the better, he added – but just to himself!

'RIGHT NOW?' Tough boomed, in the thunder that passed for his voice.

'Right now!' the Inventor replied.

'Ugh?' ugh-ed Gruff.

'Ugh!' the Inventor ugh-ed right back at him.

They set off, leaving behind a twisted poker, broken tiles, shattered eardrums and a nervous cat! The Inventor wondered, not for the first time, why he didn't employ a better class of crook!

Presently the Toughies arrived outside Mr Black's house in a van which they had 'borrowed' from a car park.

''E'll be in 'is workshop,' Rough informed the others in a whisper, as he assumed leadership in Benny's absence. (He was a little less thick than the other two!) And he led them along the path beside the house to the shed at the back where Mr Black worked on his inventions.

Mr Black, however, wasn't in the workshop. He was in the hall of his house, speaking to a friend on the telephone.

The Toughies peeked through the workshop window, saw that the hut was empty and tiptoed to the house as quietly as they could. Which wasn't very quietly! For Rough caught his neck on a clothes line and swore, Tough trod on a rake which thumped him on the face and Gruff knocked the lid off the dustbin!

These noises didn't disturb Mr Black, however, for

he was so wrapped up in his conversation that he wouldn't have heard a bomb going off just then!

'It's a shield,' he was explaining to his friend.

'But I thought it was some kind of "scanner" or "slimmer" or something?' said his friend, who was also an inventor.

'Oh, you mean the Skimmer? No, that was my *last* invention.'

'But wasn't the last one some sort of machine for making people Super?' his friend went on.

'No, that was the one *before* that. I *was* supposed to be building a new Super-machine, but ... well ... I just got carried away with this new invention and haven't got round to the old one again.'

'And you say this one's a shield? What *kind* of shield?'

'It's for making people invincible.'

'Invisible?' The telephone line wasn't too clear.

Mr Black laughed. 'No, not in*visible* – in*vincible*. For the police and the army. Knives, bullets and death-rays can't penetrate it.'

'Sounds great. Are you fetching it along to the conference?'

'Conference? What conference?'

'You know, the British Inventors' Club conference, in Edinburgh? You *are* going, aren't you?'

'Sure. Next Monday, isn't it? Don't worry, I'll be there. I'm really organized this time. I've even got a boarding house fixed up. And I'll bring the Shield, to show you all how it works ...'

'But wait a minute,' his friend cut in, 'it isn't *next*

Monday, it's *this* Monday. Tomorrow! I'm leaving right now. I'm due to catch a train in half an hour's time!'

'What?' Mr Black exploded. 'Tomorrow? In Edinburgh? I thought it was *next* week.' He paused, thoughtfully. 'I *might* just be able to catch a train to Edinburgh tonight.'

'Well I'll see you there, then,' his friend replied. 'And I *know* your Shield will be the star attraction.'

When he rang off Mr Black whirled his wheelchair round and went to his bedroom to pack a case with some clothes, pyjamas, a toothbrush and his shaving kit. Afterwards he would go outside, lock up his workshop and fetch the Shield into the house, ready to take with him to Edinburgh.

The Toughies had been standing outside the front door with their ears pressed against the opened letter-box, taking in Mr Black's every word. But now Rough decided that they had heard enough and he gestured the others away from the door.

'Let's get back to the Professor,' he whispered. 'Gotta report this to 'im.'

'WHY?' yelled Tough, in what passed as a whisper for him!

'Shush!' shushed Rough. 'Not so loud . . .'

'WHO'S BEIN' LOUD? I WAS ONLY WHISPERIN'!' Tough protested, in his usual shout.

'Ugh!' grunted Gruff, agreeing with them both, as the three of them tiptoed to their van to return to the Inventor and report Mr Black's telephone conversation.

4 The Shield – Revealed

'That was quick!' the Inventor greeted them, with a grin. 'Have you got him? Did he come quietly? Did he struggle much? Has he built another machine yet? Did you snatch it? Where is it?'

And then, when he realized that Mr Black wasn't with them, he added: 'Where is he? What have you done with him? Is he in the van?'

'We didn't bring 'im,' Rough replied. 'There wasn't no point.'

'What do you mean – you didn't bring 'im . . . I mean . . . him? There wasn't no point . . . er . . . any point?' He was beginning to turn a salmon-pink shade.

''E 'asn't built another machine. Not yet,' Rough told him.

'NO, 'E 'ASN'T!' Tough agreed, shouting.

'What's *that* got to do with it?' the Inventor bellowed. 'The idea was to kidnap him and force him to build one here, or at Benny's house, where I can get my hands on it. And where we can keep our eyes on him. You buffoons!'

When he saw the hard, glazed look which came into the Toughies' eyes, he realized that he shouldn't have called them buffoons. They were very touchy. He had to watch what he said to them.

'Er ... ah ... that is ... *plat*oons ... ah, I meant ... I said *plat*oons ...'

But Rough ignored the insult and continued: 'Yeah boss, but listen. 'E's gotta new invention, 'asn't 'e, boys?' He turned to the others who agreed with a deafening 'YEAH!' and an 'Ugh!' respectively. Then Rough went on: 'We 'eard 'im talkin' about it on the phone.'

'IT'S SOME SORTA SHIELD!' roared Tough, making the Inventor, who kept forgetting to stand back from the blast, clap his hands over his ears again.

'A shield? What sorta ... er, I mean ... what sort of shield?' He was working himself into a temper again. 'Never mind a shield. It's a Super-machine I want. Understand? A Super-machine.'

Just imagine, he fumed inwardly, sending three big, strong tough guys out to kidnap a small, weak man in a wheelchair and they come back all of a dither and nattering on about some sort of shield.

'IT'S A INVISIBLE SHIELD!' Tough thundered at him, but it was a few seconds of head-shaking before the Inventor realized what he had said.

'Invisible?' He turned to Rough for an explanation.

'Naw! Not in*visible*,' he explained scornfully, 'in – ah ... in –' He couldn't remember the word. It wasn't one that he used every day of the week! 'It's somethin' to do with Vincent ... or Vince, I think.'

'Vincent? Vince?' repeated the Inventor, still puzzled. He resolved, once he became world-ruler, to surround himself with crooks who had less brawn and more brain. Then suddenly the light dawned. 'Ah! In*vincible*? Is *that* it?'

'Yeah!' Rough's craggy face lit up.

'YEAH!' So did Tough's.

'Ugh!' Even Gruff's.

'Come on then,' the Inventor invited, 'tell me about it.'

So Rough, with a few interruptions from Tough and Gruff, repeated what they had heard of Mr Black's conversation. That the shield could withstand knives, bullets and death-rays. And that Mr Black intended taking it to the conference in Edinburgh the next day, Monday.

'What?' the Inventor exploded. 'To Edinburgh?'

'Tomorrow,' said Rough.

'To show . . . ?'

'To inventors . . . !'

'TOO BAD!' said Tough.

'Too bad? It's too-tally . . . I mean, it's totally disastrous!' the Inventor assured them.

'Why, boss?' Rough asked. 'Wha-sa-matter?'

'Wha-sa-matter? Er . . . I mean . . . what's the matter?' The Inventor's face had paled from its angry pink, but was now threatening to flare up again with frustration at the possibility of being so near to a good thing and then losing it. 'Don't you realize? This invention could be even better than the Super-machine. With an invincible shield we could block Super Gran's Super-powers and get the better of her. And then . . .' – he paused for effect – 'just think, I . . . that is, we . . .

could conquer the world. And I would be world-ruler!'

He came down to earth again. 'But this Black guy's just about to take it to show to a bunch of his pals in Edinburgh. And once he does that it won't be secret any longer and *I* won't be the only one who'll be able to use it. So we *must* get it! Now! And Black along with it, to make us dozens of them.' Already he could imagine a whole army – *his* army – being invincible behind their shields and conquering the world, for *him*!

'Now?' said Rough.

'Now,' the Inventor replied.

'RIGHT NOW?' roared Tough.

'Right now ...' The Inventor suddenly realized. 'Look, we've been through all this before!'

'Ugh!' agreed Gruff.

'Ugh!' retorted the Inventor, stealing Gruff's dialogue – and showing them the door!

Super Gran should really have cycled back to Edison's house more quickly than she did   but the cycle chain had kept coming off, as a result of her Super-pedalling. However, she reached Edison's street in time to see the Toughies' van entering from the far end, followed by a rusty old car.

The van stopped outside the Blacks' house and the Toughies jumped out and marched in single file (tall Rough, small Tough and tall Gruff) towards the gate.

'Ah-ha! I thought so!' muttered Super Gran, as she uttered, from *her* end of the street, a blood-curdling, Super-yell battle-cry!

The Toughies, about to open the gate, heard the yell and looked up. They recognized the distant, approaching figure as being Super Gran, and without hesitating they turned and fled to the van, like three actors in a speeded-up film!

They dived into their vehicle and, without even taking time to turn it round, drove it back the way they'd come, all the way up the street – in reverse gear!

Super Gran, deciding *not* to chase the Toughies, stopped at Edison's house to check that Mr Black was all right. Throwing down the bicycle, she rushed to the workshop, which he was just about to lock up.

'Sure I'm all right,' he assured her cheerily. 'Nobody's kidnapped *me*. Who would *want* to kidnap me?'

'The Inventor, for one,' she informed him grimly. 'His gang was right outside this house one minute ago!'

He couldn't believe it. 'But why would they want to kidnap me?'

'They must be after your new Super-machine,' the old lady suggested. 'You know, the one I gave you the money to build? The one I *keep* giving you the money to build!'

'Oh ... ah ... um ... *that* one?' he stammered.

Super Gran frowned at him and then, suspecting something, she quickly read his mind. 'Ah, so that's it! You haven't *built* a new Super-machine yet!'

'Er ... ah ... well no, not quite. I *was* going to, but ... you see ...'

'Didn't Edison give you the reward money to build

it? The money I got for getting yon Arabs their Crown Jewels back?' She had given Edison most of the reward money (keeping back just a small amount for a rainy day), on the understanding that her father would rebuild the Super-machine.

'Oh yes, she did. It's just that ... well ... you see ...'

'See what? What did you do with it?' She stood, arms akimbo, feet apart, glowering down at him sitting in his wheelchair outside the workshop, feeling like a schoolmistress ticking off a small, naughty boy. 'You *did* use it for something? But not for the Super-machine, is that it?'

Mr Black, his fingers idly fiddling with one of the chair's wheels, suddenly looked up at her with a bashful grin on his face – looking just like the small, naughty schoolboy she had just imagined him to be. 'I've got a new invention,' he said proudly.

Super Gran frowned disapprovingly. 'Not again! You said that before, and the last time it was yon Skimmer. So what is it *this* time, may I ask? What's the invention that takes priority over a new Super-machine? Eh?'

Mr Black, going ahead in his chair, opened the door and led the way into his workshop. He pointed to an object standing in a corner which was about one and a half metres high and made of thick blue-tinted plastic; it was curved like a bow-window, was dome-topped, and had two handles inside for holding it.

'Oh aye?' Super Gran, unimpressed, inspected it. 'So that's what the hard-earned reward money was spent

43

on, was it?' She inspected it again to see if she had missed anything the first time round. But she hadn't! 'And what does it do, exactly?'

She clearly thought that this insignificant object wasn't worth a fraction of the money which had been spent on making it. 'What does it do?' she repeated. 'Not a lot, by the look of it!'

'That's what *you* think! I'll show you!' Mr Black wheeled his chair to the corner, took hold of the Shield by its internal handles and held it in front of him. 'Now, try punching it,' he challenged. 'Or kicking it. Or karate-chopping it. Or anything you like. Go on, try it . . .'

'But – my Super-powers, laddie!' the old lady laughed. 'Have you forgotten them?' She didn't want to shatter his dreams *or* his Shield. And especially the Shield, for the flying fragments of pulverized plastic might injure him.

But the proud inventor, the grinning Mr Black, shook his head. 'Don't worry! This is the answer to *all* your Super-powers!'

'What?' She was insulted. 'That wee bit o' plastic?'

'Go on then, try it and see,' he challenged her again. 'I guarantee I'll be safe sitting here behind it.'

Eventually she was persuaded to carry out the tests. She punched it, gently at first, then harder as she realized it could withstand her Super-punches. 'Jings! You're right!' she exclaimed. 'It *is* Super Gran-proof!'

She kicked it, she karate-chopped it and she shoulder-charged it – but it remained intact. And poor old

44

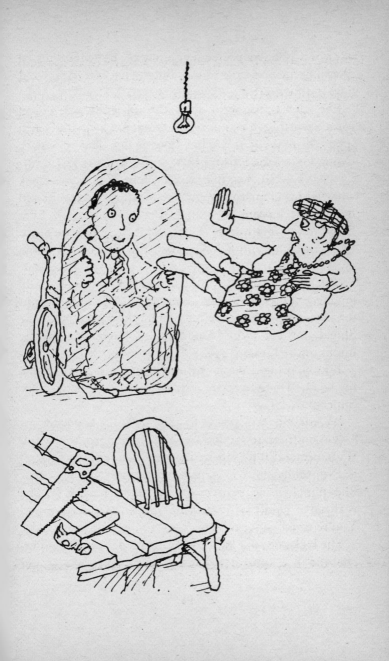

Super Gran ended up with a sore fist, foot, hand and shoulder!

She tried one final punch at it, but, in her frustration, her swing went wild and she smashed the light-bulb above her head. 'Havers!' she exclaimed in exasperation.

'Oh, don't worry about that. I'll get it fixed afterwards,' he assured her, dismissing the problem.

'Now try and read my mind through it,' he further challenged her.

'Read your mind? That's easy-peasy!' She put her hands to her temples and concentrated hard on the man's thoughts. But again without success. Her mind-reading wasn't working either!

Then Mr Black put the Shield to one side, and he thought: I *told* you the Shield would defeat your powers, didn't I?

'Aye, you're right, laddie, you did,' Super Gran said, in answer to the man's unspoken thoughts. At which he grinned, knowing that she *had* read his mind that time.

Next, he whispered as quietly as he could with his back to her, and she heard him quite easily with her Super-hearing. But when he repeated the test behind the Shield she couldn't hear a word, even when he shouted.

'That's certainly some invention you've got there,' Super Gran enthused, admitting that it seemed to be exactly what he claimed it to be – the answer to all her Super-powers. 'And just think of all the things it could be used for. A safety glass in cars, for instance . . .'

'The whole *car* could be made of it,' Mr Black corrected.

'Whole buildings even, in earthquake countries,' Super Gran said.

'Or riot shields for the police, a defensive weapon for armies . . .'

'In aircraft and ships . . .'

'In spacecraft . . .'

They were too busy listing all the Shield's possible uses to notice the Inventor creeping silently away from the window. He had seen enough. He had seen the tests which Super Gran had carried out on the Shield and *he* was as pleased with it as *they* were. And he meant to have it for himself.

When Super Gran had chased the Toughies out of the street she hadn't noticed that the rusty old car which had followed the van into the street and quietly parked farther along the road was the Inventor's! And when Super Gran had entered Mr Black's garden the Inventor had followed her to find out for himself about Black's Shield.

And now that he had seen it in action, he was more determined than ever to have it before anyone else knew about it. And especially before the other inventors at Edinburgh could inspect it and copy it.

There was no point in trying to do anything about it there and then. Not against Super Gran! He knew better than that! He had tangled with her before and had come off worst!

No, he would round up his gang, and Rough could keep Super Gran occupied while Tough snatched Mr Black and Gruff snatched the Shield.

He drove to his house to reorganize his forces . . .

5 Wheelies with a Wheelchair

Mr Black suddenly remembered that he was due in Edinburgh at eleven o'clock the next morning for the conference.

'Then you'll have to get a move on if you want to catch a train tonight, laddie,' Super Gran nagged him.

She closed the shutters on the workshop window as Mr Black went to lock the door, having removed the Shield.

'Oh, I've left the keys in the house,' he muttered. 'Never mind, I'll lock it on my way out.' He crossed the garden with Super Gran, going towards the house.

'I'll find out about the trains while you get ready,' the old lady offered, 'and I'll tell the lassie where you've gone when she gets home.' She knew that Edison wouldn't be there for hours yet!

She phoned the station and was told that the last connecting train for Edinburgh was due to leave Chisleton in twenty minutes.

The problem was: how to get Mr Black to the station? His wheelchair made it impossible to go by bus. '*And* I've got the Shield to take, as well as my suitcase,' he reminded Super Gran.

'A taxi?' she suggested, reaching for the phone again.

But she was told that the taxis were all out and the first one wasn't due back inside half an hour.

As time was passing there was nothing else for it – she would have to *push* him to the station! But that was no problem for Super Gran.

She lifted the Shield and placed it over Mr Black as he sat in his wheelchair, his small overnight case resting on his knees. She put it over him so that it stood outside his feet on the chair's foot-rest, fitting around him and up past his head.

'That's the easiest way to carry it,' she said.

They set off, but in their hurry Mr Black forgot, after all, to lock the workshop. Grimly gripping the small suitcase between his knees, he grasped the Shield with one hand and grabbed at the side of the chair with the other, to hold on for dear life!

For when Super Gran pushed the wheelchair she did it at her usual Super-speed! She whizzed down the garden path and along the pavement, zooming towards the station.

'Here goes! Hold tight!' she warned as they started out – as if her passenger needed to be told!

The journey didn't take long. It wouldn't, not with Super Gran at the helm!

The only thing was, she zoomed round a corner out of the High Street too quickly for a jogger who was heading towards them. She swerved the chair to avoid him and the jogger moved in the same direction; then she swerved it the other way and the jogger did the same. Then, during one last swerve – because she and

50

the chair were travelling too fast – the inevitable happened. This final manoeuvre was one too many and the wheelchair tipped over sideways, throwing Mr Black, his suitcase and the Shield along the top of a roughcast wall, into a large clump of thorny bushes!

'Ow! Ouch!' Mr Black yelled, with fright rather than pain.

'Are you all right?' Super Gran hauled him, his Shield and his suitcase from the bushes, shuddering at the thought of the breaks and bruises he must have received, being scraped and prickled at *that* speed. She scolded herself and resolved not to go so fast in future.

'But I'm all right!' Mr Black revealed, not unduly surprised. For he had confidence that the Shield would protect him. Which it *had* done. There was not a mark on *him*, and there were only a few tiny scratches on the Shield.

'It *does* work, doesn't it?' Super Gran confirmed, as she helped him back into the chair and replaced the Shield and suitcase, ready to resume their journey – but more slowly this time!

Meanwhile the Inventor had persuaded the three Toughies to have another go at kidnapping Mr Black and the Shield. With the Shield – or, better still, with hundreds of Shields – he could go ahead with his world-conquering plans without having to fear further intervention from Super Gran and her Super-powers.

He could have gone with the Toughies, but decided not to. If Super Gran was no longer there, they'd be able to snatch Black and the Shield without his help. And if Super Gran *was* still there, then he, the Inventor, might get hurt!

As Benny's boys drove once more to Edison's house, Rough reminded the others of the previous occasion when the Inventor and Benny had tried to kidnap Super Gran and had made a mess of it.

'They snatched the *wrong* li'l ol' lady!' Rough said, in his usual rough, rasping, sandpaper voice. They had kidnapped Mrs Preston, Super Gran's friend, in error.

'YEAH!' Tough thundered, 'IMAGINE DOIN' ANYTHIN' SO DAFT!'

'Ugh!' muttered Gruff, the driver, in agreement.

'There's no chance of *us* doin' that, is there?' Rough guffawed.

'NO CHANCE!' Tough agreed.

'Ugh!' Gruff uttered again, also presumably in agreement.

By rights, Edison shouldn't have arrived home for hours yet, at the painfully slow rate she cycled. But one of the Meals on Wheels vans had passed and the driver, feeling sorry for her and recognizing her as a friend of Super Gran, had stopped to give her and her bicycle a lift home. With the result that she arrived only a few minutes before the Toughies.

Thinking that her father and Super Gran would be in the workshop, Edison made straight for it. She opened the unlocked door and walked into the darkness created by the shuttered window. Then she switched on the light, found that the bulb was 'gone', tried to move further into the hut, stumbled – as usual! – over a box of tools, and went sprawling towards a chair, which crashed to the floor under her.

And it was just as she was trying to scramble to her feet again in the darkness that the three Toughies descended on her with a large, dirty sack ... !

'That was quick!' the Inventor greeted them, for the second time that afternoon, with a big grin. 'Have you got him *this* time? Did he come quietly? Did he struggle much? Did you get the Shield? Where's his wheelchair?'

'Yus, no, yus, no – and dunno,' replied Rough to the Inventor's five questions.

'What?' The Inventor repeated the questions and ticked them off on his fingers: 'Yes, you've got him. No, he *didn't* come quietly. Yes, he *did* struggle a lot. No, you *didn't* get the Shield – why not? And where's the wheelchair – you dunno? I mean ... er ... you don't know?'

'COULDN'T FIND NO SHIELD,' Tough blasted at him. 'IT WAS DARK IN THAT THERE 'UT. THE SHUTTERS WAS UP.'

'Yeah,' Rough agreed, 'an' we didn't see no wheel-chair, neither. 'E was just sorta lyin' in an 'eap on the floor, see? An' we just shoved this 'ere sack over 'is 'ead ...'

'You *could* have put the light on,' the Inventor pointed out, having by this time recovered from Tough's extended shout. It *had* been rather a long speech, for Tough, and it had been rather tough – on the Inventor's ears!

'DIDN'T THINK OF IT,' Tough admitted.

'Ugh!' said Gruff, which meant that he hadn't thought of it either!

Meanwhile, the sack containing the supposed Mr Black was thrashing about violently on the floor, where the Toughies had deposited it. And from it came the muffled but decidedly high-pitched screams which told the Inventor that something was amiss. Or rather, that something was *a Miss*!

He was *sure* that Black's voice should be lower-pitched than that! So *who*, he wondered, had been given the sack! Untying the knot which secured the neck, he pulled the string apart – and Edison's head popped out, still screaming!

'What the ...?' The Inventor was momentarily speechless. '*This* isn't Black!'

'We ... we can see that,' Rough nodded, taken aback and giggling slightly with embarrassment.

'IT'S THE GIRL!' announced Tough, who was quick where things like that were concerned!

'Ugh!' muttered Gruff, who was also quick!

They had done it again. They were fated! The Inventor, Benny and the Toughies just weren't cut out to be kidnappers! First of all the Inventor and Benny had blundered, and now the Toughies.

At that moment Benny arrived, his other 'job' having been carried out. But his entrance went unnoticed, the other four baddies being too busy shouting about each other's incompetence to bother about who had, or hadn't, entered the room.

'You stupid nits . . .' the Inventor was yelling, which was rather brave of him in the circumstances.

'WOT WAS THAT?' Tough grabbed him by the collar, hoisted him into the air and glowered threateningly at him, his fist poised to make an impression on the Inventor's nose!

Einstein the cat looked up idly from a position of safety – under the table – at the suspended Inventor and the glaring Tough. What, he wondered, were these crazy humans up to now? They seemed to be assaulting each other again!

'Hi . . . guys!' Benny greeted them, and, 'Hi . . . boss!' he added, to his high boss. 'Enjoyin' yourselves?' He looked from the elevated Inventor and the Toughies to the sackful of Edison sitting screaming on the floor. ''Ello, wot's . . . the girl . . . doin' 'ere . . . ?'

The Inventor looked down from his lofty position in Tough's grasp. 'They were supposed' – choke, choke, – 'to kidnap Black' – choke, choke, – 'not his daughter' – choke, choke, – 'they kidnapped' – choke, choke, – 'the wrong person!' – choke, choke.

'Yeah, but so did you an' Benny, last time,' Rough reminded them.

'Ugh!' Gruff grunted in agreement. He even nodded vigorously, to add conviction to his grunt!

'*Who* did?' Benny demanded, '. . . like?'

'YOU DID, LIKE!' Tough roared in reply, accident-ally tightening his grip on the Inventor's neck in his excitement.

'Ugh!' choked the Inventor.

'Ugh?' protested Gruff. The Inventor was stealing his dialogue again!

'But anyway ... the boys ...' Benny pointed out, 'couldn't 'ave ... snatched the ... Black man ... like ...'

'Wot black man?' Rough asked, frowning. 'We weren't supposed to snatch no black man!'

'The *Black* ... man – *Mr* Black – wasn't ... at 'ome ... was 'e?'

Tough dropped the Inventor to the floor. 'Y? Ware was 'e?' the Inventor croaked as he massaged his neck and glared at Tough, correcting it eventually to: 'Why? Where was he?'

''E was ... at the ... station,' Benny informed them. ''E an' ... that there ... Super Gran ... came whizzin' ... up at ... fifty miles ... an hour. Goin' somewhere ... 'e was ...'

'Going somewhere?' the Inventor murmured.

''E 'ad ... a suitcase an' ... a sorta ... blue shield ... thing ...'

'Suitcase? Shield?' the Inventor interrupted, spluttering. 'Edinburgh! That's where he was going! Edinburgh!'

'Edin ... burgh ... ?' It was Benny's turn to look puzzled.

The Inventor nodded. 'I'll tell you all about it later.'

'But ... but I ... know about ... it, like,' Benny beamed.

'You do?' The Inventor couldn't understand how Benny could know about the afternoon's happenings when he hadn't been there.

'Yeah! It's . . . in Scot-land . . . isn't it . . . ?'

'I didn't mean *that*! I meant . . . oh, never mind, I'll tell you about it afterwards. Meanwhile, *we're* going there!' He suddenly looked determined. The Shield was about to slip out of his grasp. 'We're going after Black . . .'

6   (Ar)rivals in Edinburgh!

'After Black?' Benny said. 'Where . . . to, like?'

'Edinburgh.'

'Edin . . . burgh?'

'Edinburgh!'

'But it's . . . in Scot-land . . . like.'

'That's right,' the Inventor agreed.

'But . . . why?' Benny asked.

'Because the capital of Scotland can't be in England . . . Oh, I see what you mean! Well anyway, we've got to get after Black. He's got the Shield with him, to show to those other inventors. And we're going to snatch it off him.'

'Shield? In . . . ventors?' Benny, knowing nothing of Mr Black's phone conversation, looked blank – as usual!

The Inventor gave him a brief, hurried account of the afternoon's happenings, then phoned the station for the times of the trains and turned to his gang: 'I want you all to go home and pack a toothbrush, pyjamas, a razor and . . .'

'Toothbrush? Wot for?' Rough interrupted him. '*I* don't use no toothbrush!'

'PYJAMAS?' roared Tough, 'I DON'T USE NO PYJAMAS!'

Before Gruff's 'Ugh!' could be translated to indicate

that he didn't use a toothbrush, or pyjamas – or both! – Benny broke in on the discussion (which made a change from breaking in on houses!).

'Hey!' he yelled excitedly. 'Where's the . . . girl? She's . . . scarpered, like . . . !'

'I'LL GO AFTER 'ER,' Tough volunteered, but the Inventor stopped him:

'Don't bother. It's her father we want.'

Benny was still puzzled about the whole thing. 'But . . . wot did . . . you want . . . 'er for . . . anyway?'

'I *didn't*,' the Inventor explained. 'These stupid nits snatched the wrong one . . .' Oh-oh, he'd said it again!

Tough grabbed him.

'Oh no!' the Inventor croaked. 'Here' – choke, choke, – 'we go' – choke, choke, – 'again!' – choke, choke.

'Ugh! Ugh!' said Gruff. Which was *his* version of 'You can say *that* again!'

While the men were arguing, Edison had taken the chance to climb quickly out of the sack, tiptoe from the room and sneak quietly out of the house. At least she *meant* to sneak out quickly and quietly but unfortunately, being Edison, she couldn't do anything without tripping over her feet. Although, to be fair, the Inventor's old garden wheelbarrow, rusting among the weeds near the front door, contributed to her downfall! She landed on her face immediately beneath the window of the room from which she had just sneaked.

Which was fortunate. For she lay there, hardly daring

61

to breathe in case of discovery, and listened to the Inventor and company discussing their journey to Edinburgh.

When she had heard enough she crawled along past the window until it was safe for her to stand up. Then she jumped to her feet and ran as fast as she could for home, tripping only once on the way!

'They're going to catch the first train to Edinburgh tomorrow,' she told Super Gran and Willard, when she met them at her house. 'They're going after Dad – and the Shield!'

'What'll we do now, Gran?' asked Willard.

'We'll have to go after them. And stop them!' she replied determinedly. 'We've got to protect Edison's Dad – and his Shield.'

'To Edinburgh?' Willard said, astonished.

'Sure laddie, why not?'

'*All* of us?' Edison exclaimed.

'Well, lassie, it's like this – Willie's parents are away on a golf outing to St Annes and I'm baby-sitting for them . . .'

'Huh! Baby-sitting!' Willard interrupted, snorting. 'Me? A baby? Huh!'

'So I can't leave him behind,' Super Gran continued. 'And I'm sure *you'll* want to go, to keep your eye on your Dad?'

Edison nodded, but looked thoughtful. If they caught the same train as the Inventor and company and Super Gran tackled them, other passengers might get hurt in the resulting punch-up. And besides, although Super

Gran was Super – was she a match for four big tough hoodlums and a medium-sized coward (the Inventor!) in the close confines of a moving train?

'Aye, you're quite right,' Super Gran broke in on the girl's thoughts. 'The train's *not* the place for a wee punch-up, is it?' Then she tut-tutted and shook her head. 'But I'm ashamed of you! How could you think I'd possibly *lose*?'

'Hey Gran, what was all *that* about?' Willard asked, bewildered.

She explained what she had read in Edison's mind, and went on: 'No, we want to get to Edinburgh ahead of them and avoid a punch-up. Pity though!' She would have preferred a good fight!

'Oh, Super Gran,' Edison scolded her, 'you *are* awful!'

'Aye, I know, lassie!' Super Gran giggled.

'But how do we get there?' the boy nagged, eager to get on with it. Too much talk and too little action bored Willard. And besides, he had never been to Scotland and was curious to find out if everyone up there wore kilts!

'Now, let's see,' Super Gran said thoughtfully, 'I've still got some of that reward money left, haven't I? From the Arabs?'

'Yes, Super Gran, but you were keeping it for an emergency.'

'Aye, but this *is* an emergency,' she replied, 'so we'll use it. We'll fly there!'

'Fly there?' Willard gasped, his eyes almost popping from his head. 'Don't tell me you can *fly*, Gran?'

Super Gran giggled and shook her head. 'Afraid not, laddie. Who do you think I am? I'm Super *Gran*, not Super*man*!' She laughed again, and explained: 'No, we'll go by plane like everyone else does – and get there before those five scunners arrive.'

'Gran, what *is* a "scunner"?' Willard asked, but Super Gran, too busy with thoughts of her travel plans, didn't hear the question.

'Aye, we'll pack some things, take the bus from Chisleton to the airport and get the first stand-by flight to Edinburgh. Nae bother at a'!'

But it wasn't 'no bother at all'. By the time they got to the airport the last flight had gone. So they had to spend the night in a boarding-house and get up early the next morning in time to catch the first flight out at half-past seven.

They arrived at Turnhouse Airport, Edinburgh, just over an hour later and Edison, being Edison, tripped on the way down the aircraft steps on to Scottish soil.

'Enjoy your trip to Scotland!' Willard guffawed, as she picked herself up and glowered at him.

While travelling into the city on the bus Willard kept looking out for Scotsmen wearing kilts. Super Gran explained that wearing '*the* kilt' was the proper expression, rather than wearing '*a* kilt'. But this just made Willard imagine *one* kilt, worn by *everyone*, at *once*! And when Super Gran read his mind and told Edison about it, all three of them laughed at the idea of one gigantic kilt surrounding thousands of Scotsmen!

Mr Black's train had been delayed by maintenance

work for almost four hours, so Super Gran and company arrived at the airport city terminal, near Waverley Station, just as the train arrived at the platform.

'Hi Dad!' Edison greeted him as he wheeled his way along the platform to the barrier.

'What . . . ? What are *you* lot doing here?' He couldn't believe his eyes. 'And how did you *get* here?'

'We flew!' Willard informed him.

'What? Don't tell me you can *fly*, Super Gran?' he laughed.

'She's Super *Gran*, not Super*man*!' the children yelled, in chorus.

'We've been through all that before,' the old lady grinned, as Edison took the Shield from her father and carried it.

'But what are you all doing here?' he demanded.

'I'll tell you afterwards,' Super Gran promised, as she grabbed his wheelchair and pushed it to the exit.

'Okay. But don't push so hard this time!' Mr Black warned her. 'It took all night for my nerves to recover from our last trip!'

'We'll need to find somewhere to stay,' Super Gran said, as she guided the wheelchair up the slope out of the station.

'That's no problem,' Mr Black assured her. 'You can all come to *my* place. It's a friend's boarding-house, you see. An old army pal, John Anderson.' He pointed to a phone box. 'I'll just check that it's all right to bring you.'

Edison put the Shield down, dialled the number and

held the phone out of the box towards her father so that he could use it. But his friend, it seemed, was in London on business and the boarding-house was being looked after by his old mother.

'Have you got room for another three?' Mr Black asked her, after he had introduced himself and explained about the others.

'Sure, sure. No bother, you ken. Come along any time,' he was told.

'Are you positive?' he insisted. It all sounded too easy. She hadn't taken time to look up registers or diaries and had said yes right away without thinking or checking, apparently.

'Och, don't worry,' Super Gran said cheerily. 'We'll go along and see for ourselves while you're at the conference. If she hasn't got room we can always go somewhere else.'

As Edison replaced the phone in the box Mr Black fished a dirty, crumpled piece of paper out of his pocket. 'Here's the address. You three go on there. I'll take a taxi to the conference.'

'Dad, the Shield!' Edison reminded him, swapping it for his suitcase, which she would carry to the house, along with their own cases.

While Super Gran pushed the wheelchair to the nearest taxi-rank she warned Mr Black that the Inventor and his mob were on their way. 'Make sure you leave that Shield gadget with the officials at the conference. Get them to lock it up somewhere safe.'

And so, while Mr Black's taxi travelled west along

Princes Street, Edinburgh's main thoroughfare, Super Gran and company headed north, crossing *over* Princes Street. They walked up and over the hill, past the bus station and round a couple of corners until, after about half a mile, they reached the boarding-house.

'There's four of you, is there?' old Mrs Anderson greeted them presently, in surprise. 'I wasn't expecting as many as that, you ken!' She laughed. 'I couldn't understand the man's English accent – so I just agreed with everything he said!'

She was a small, round, fat, cheery old soul but she wasn't used to running the boarding-house, except in an emergency, and she wasn't really up to it.

'I thought the *man* was coming along?' she said, puzzled.

'Aye, later,' Super Gran confirmed. 'And ... eh ... ah ... our rooms?'

'Well,' the old woman began, 'I've got one room on the ground floor – the man's in a wheelchair, did you say? Then that should be all right for him, eh? And you can go in with him, can't you, sonny?' she turned to Willard.

'Sure,' the boy nodded, wondering when they would get something to eat. He was starving.

'And there's another spare room for you two – I think!' She hesitated thoughtfully. 'Aye, it'll be all right. Two floors up.' She took her glasses out of her overall pocket, she put them on, she looked at the register, she turned the pages back and forth a few times; then finally she declared: 'Och aye, that'll be all right. I'm

68

sure it will. Sure.' And she returned her glasses to her pocket.

Super Gran wondered if she should read the old woman's mind to find out why there seemed to be some doubt about the room. But the landlady continued:

'Are you here for the Games?'

'Games? What Games?'

'At Meadowbank,' the old woman explained. 'The British Games, you ken. At Meadowbank Sports Centre.'

'Oh yes,' Edison confirmed, 'I saw a big banner near the station advertising them.'

The old woman nodded. 'They're on all this week. The town's mobbed. You're lucky to *get* a room. Luckily I've got a spare one. At least . . .' She hesitated, thinking it over. 'At least, I *think* I've got a spare room, you ken.' She saw Super Gran and Edison exchanging worried glances, and added hastily: 'Och, I'm *sure* it'll be all right. It's just that . . . well, *your* room belongs to Wilfred, a salesman from Manchester. He's up here every few months looking for sales in Edinburgh and the Borders area. But he's away at the Borders just now. So you can have *his* room. He won't be back till Saturday.'

'That's all right then,' Super Gran smiled, with relief, 'we'll be away by Friday.'

'The only thing is . . .' Mrs Anderson began again hesitantly.

Now what? Super Gran thought.

'It's just a wee thing, you ken. But he's taken his room key with him by mistake, so you won't be able to lock your door.' She frowned, then smiled cheerily. 'But I don't suppose that'll bother you, eh?'

Super Gran shook her head. 'Och! That's no bother. As long as we get a room, that's the main thing. A key doesn't matter.'

7 Super Gran Goes by Bus!

'And now, would you like something to eat?' the old woman asked, after they'd put their cases into their rooms.

The famished Willard had been thinking she'd *never* ask! 'Sure thing!' he said.

'It's a pity you're too late for breakfast,' Mrs Anderson told them, 'or you could've had a big plate of Scotch porridge . . .'

'Oh no!' There was a shriek from Super Gran. 'Not porridge!'

Mrs Anderson was taken aback. 'But I thought you *were* Scottish and you'd *like* porridge?'

'I am and I did – but I don't now,' Super Gran groaned. 'I had enough of the stuff recently to last me for years! Yeugh!'

The children laughed, remembering how in London they'd had to force her to eat it, to make her failing Super-powers return.

And so, instead of porridge, they sat down to fish fingers, chips and peas, followed by a strawberry-flavoured instant dessert and tinned fruit, followed by tea and biscuits.

When Mrs Anderson was clearing away the dirty

dishes, Super Gran noticed a large, red, angry-looking weal on the old woman's hand.

'I burned it on the pan,' she explained. 'Och, it's nothing, you ken. Don't worry about it.'

But Super Gran and Edison could see that it looked sore and must *feel* sore.

'You won't be able to wash the dishes with that,' Super Gran said. 'You don't want to put your hand into hot water.'

'I'll just have to,' the old woman said, grimacing.

'Blethers!' Super Gran exclaimed. '*I'll* do them for you!'

'You?'

'Aye! I'll have them done for you before my Sassenach friends here' – she nodded towards Edison and Willard – 'can say "it's a braw bricht, moon-licht, nicht the nicht"! Just show me where the kitchen is and leave everything to Super Gran.'

'Super Gran?' the old woman said. 'I saw you'd signed that in the visitors' book – but I didn't know what it meant.'

'You mean – you've never heard of me?' Super Gran was shocked that her fame seemed not to have reached Edinburgh yet.

Mrs Anderson led the way into the kitchen as all four of them (Willard somewhat reluctantly!) carried the dirty dishes there. And what happened after that was more of a blur than anything else. The landlady could only stand and stare, her mouth open in amazement.

Super Gran poured the hot water and the washing-up liquid into the sink – which was all she did at normal speed! For after that she washed the dishes like lightning, and dried them like Super-lightning! And sixty seconds after she had started, she was finished!

'Right then, that's that!' she exclaimed, as she put the piles of gleaming crockery into a cupboard and the shining cutlery into a drawer. 'Is there anything else?' She looked round. 'Oh aye, the pots and pans.'

Seconds later they too were gleaming. By which time Mrs Anderson had flopped down on to a kitchen chair, shattered.

'Jings!' she muttered. 'Now I've seen *everything*!'

'What? That was *nothing*!' Super Gran boasted. 'I can do a lot more than that, can't I?' She appealed to the children who stood in the kitchen doorway, giggling. 'I can run, jump, fight and lift heavy things and I can see, hear, swim, row boats, whistle and ... och ... everything!'

'Jings!' the landlady muttered again. 'Can you really?'

'Of course I can. I can do ...' She stopped.

'*Any*thing!' the children finished for her, in chorus.

'I'll give you a demonstration right now, if you like?' she offered.

Before Mrs Anderson could reply, Super Gran had opened the back door of the kitchen. The garden was just a small lawn surrounded on its three sides by walls about two metres high.

She jumped down the three steps into the grassy area and she pointed to the back wall facing her. 'See that

73

wall?' She turned to Mrs Anderson, who had followed her out of the house, along with Willard and Edison. 'I'll jump it!'

'You couldn't!' the old woman gasped.

'You *shouldn't*!' Edison warned.

'Nonsense, lassie! Here goes!' She ran forward, leapt into the air, cleared the wall and . . .

'Oh-oh!' Mrs Anderson cried out, suddenly remembering. 'Oh no!'

'Oh no – what?' asked Edison, in alarm.

'I just remembered . . . !' The old woman put her hand to her mouth fearfully.

'Remembered what?' Edison demanded.

When they heard the dull thud at the other side of the wall, fear gripped the children's hearts. What had happened to Super Gran?

They looked round, saw that there was no door or gate or other way out of the garden and looked back towards the house.

'Come on,' Willard urged, running ahead. 'We'll have to go this way . . .'

They ran through the kitchen, through the hall and out the front door to the street. And for once Edison, behind Willard, didn't take time to trip!

Outside in the street they turned left, ran a few metres to the corner of the building and turned left again into a steep, hilly side-street alongside the boarding-house. Then they ran downhill to reach the street at the back of the house, which, they discovered, lay at a much lower level than the street at the front of the house.

74

On seeing a double-decker bus standing at the side of the road they stopped, fearing the worst! For Super Gran had jumped from the safety of a back garden – into a main street!

The children stood motionless, looking all over for a sign of Super Gran, who was nowhere in sight. And then:

'Coo-ee! Will-ard! Edi-son!' It was *her* voice, all right. But where was it coming from?

Fearfully and hesitantly Willard and Edison bent down to look under the bus. And then, seeing no one there, they walked round to the front where they saw the driver standing outside his cab – looking upwards. They followed his gaze.

'I heard the thump!' he explained, scratching his head, puzzled.

'Up here!' Super Gran's voice wafted down to them. She stood up – on top of the bus, where she had landed! – and waved to them. 'I didn't know the wall had a big drop on this side!' she laughed.

The driver stared in amazement. He had never seen anything like it before. Had anyone? He didn't often have little old ladies on the top *deck* of his bus – never mind on its *roof*!

'But I'm not an ordinary little old lady,' she explained, reading his mind. 'I'm Super Gran, you see!'

Meanwhile, Mr Black had arrived at the conference hall to discover that, because of a fire, the meetings had been transferred to Leith Town Hall, starting the

next day, Tuesday, at eleven o'clock. So there was nothing else for it but to tell the driver to take him to his boarding-house.

Presently, as the taxi on its return journey along Princes Street waited to turn at the traffic lights, its occupant was spotted – and recognized.

'Look! There's Black, in that taxi!' cried the Inventor excitedly.

He and his gang had recently surfaced from the depths of Waverley Station. They had found out where the conference was taking place and were on their way there when, luckily for them, Mr Black had been sighted.

''E's got . . . the Shield . . . with 'im, Professor,' Benny said.

'Yes, and that'll save us going along to the conference and pinching it in public,' the Inventor beamed. His luck was in. 'Come on, let's find a taxi.'

They scrambled across the road between the traffic and were fortunate to find a vacant, cruising taxi just as Mr Black's vehicle turned off Princes Street. They clambered aboard, each of the five shoving the other four aside, with the Inventor, naturally, coming off worst and getting in last!

'Follow that car! That taxi! Quick!' he yelled at the driver, thereby achieving one of his life's *lesser* ambitions. He had always wanted to say that to someone, and now he had! Almost everyone he had ever seen in films got to say it sooner or later, so why shouldn't he?

He leant forward towards the driver, partly to give

instructions and partly to avoid the crush in the back of the cab, where Benny and the three Toughies took up most of the space, leaving only about a square centimetre for him!

'WHERE WE GOIN'?' Tough shouted. In the taxi's confined space, he almost shattered the Inventor's eardrums!

'We're ... following ... that ... taxi,' the Inventor explained, spitting out one word at a time as he thumped his ears to clear them!

'Yeah, but why?' Rough demanded.

The Inventor sighed. 'We couldn't kidnap Black and snatch the Shield out there in the open, in full view of everyone, right in the centre of Edinburgh. Now could we?'

The Toughies nodded wisely in agreement.

'Plus the fact,' the Inventor continued, slowly and clearly, 'that *he* was in a taxi and *we* were *not* in a taxi. Therefore *we* couldn't catch up with *him* until *we* also got in a taxi. Right?'

'Right!' they agreed.

It was like reading Goldilocks to the Three Bears!

'So we follow him to his lodgings and grab him there. Or at least, we grab the Shield. Okay?'

'Okay! Good ... idea, boss,' said Benny.

'Yes, *I* think so, too!' the Inventor agreed, modestly.

However, when Mr Black arrived at the boarding-house, Willard, Edison and Super Gran (having descended from the top of the bus!) were there to help him, his wheelchair and his Shield out of the taxi.

78

'Curses!' muttered the Inventor, 'Super Gran! What's *she* doing here? And how did she *get* here?'

'Maybe she ... flew, like?' Benny suggested.

'Who do you think she is? She's Super *Gran*, not Super*man*!' his boss scowled.

He noted the address of the boarding-house and told the driver to drive past it, back to the city centre. They would return later.

As the taxi sped away only Edison noticed it. The others were listening to Mr Black telling them of the conference's change of venue.

'Super Gran ... !' Edison caught the old lady's arm. 'That looked like the Inventor and his gang in that taxi!'

'Where?' Super Gran spun round, but the vehicle had already turned a corner.

'It's gone!' Edison cried. 'But I'm *sure* it was them.'

'Well if it was, that means they know where we're staying,' Super Gran murmured thoughtfully.

'What'll we do?' Edison looked worried.

'We'll just have to keep our eyes open – and our doors locked!'

But locking *their* bedroom door that night was impossible, as Wilfred the salesman was away with the key! When Mrs Anderson had told them about this it didn't seem to matter too much. But now it did. For they had the Shield to guard!

'Your Dad had better take it into *his* room,' Super Gran suggested as they prepared for bed. 'Seeing that *his* door locks.'

'Yes, and *we* had better jam our door shut with a chair. Just in case!' Edison replied.

'Och! You don't have to worry when you've got *me* to protect you!' Super Gran said huffily. No one needed a locked door when *she* was around!

'Yes, but we've had a long day. You're tired. You need your sleep,' said Edison, as she jammed a chair-back under the door knob, just in case!

Edison was soon asleep and dreaming. And she was dreaming that she, Willard, Super Gran, her Dad, his wheelchair and his Shield were all on top of a bus and were being chased by the Inventor and his mob in a taxi, careering along the main road at a reckless speed. Then it changed, as dreams suddenly do, and she found that she was being pursued by the Toughies, who kept throwing a sack over her head.

She awoke in a cold sweat, panicking. She looked towards the other bed in the room, saw Super Gran there (and heard her snoring!) and felt relieved and comforted. She was safe after all.

But then she slowly became aware of a slight noise on the landing. A creaking floorboard! Footsteps! The door knob being turned! A scrabbling sound near the keyhole . . .

There was someone out there – and that someone was trying to get in!

8   Midnight Madness

'Super Gran!' Edison whispered urgently, as she leapt in one bound from under her bedclothes and across the space between the two beds to grab the old lady's arm.

'Whasssup . . . ? Who-is-it . . . ?' Super Gran gasped. She shot up in bed and her hands automatically took up a karate stance!

'Shhhhhh!' Edison shushed, putting her hand over Super Gran's mouth. 'Someone's trying to get in!'

The door was being rattled and shaken and the thought which struck them both was: 'That scunnery Inventor and his mob!'

Super Gran, like the recent – and unexpected – 'Super'-Edison, shot out of bed and over to the door. Without stopping to think, she yanked the chair away from under the door handle, hauled the door open and, still without stopping – or thinking! – launched herself at the person who was standing just outside on the landing.

She caught him round the legs and her momentum carried them both to the edge of – and over – the stairs. Then, locked together, they clattered down the complete flight to the first-floor landing; they wrestled across this and clattered right down the next flight to the ground-floor hallway!

The yells, shouts, thuds and thumps brought Edison, Willard, Mr Black in his wheelchair (eventually) and the other guests out of their respective rooms in their respective nightwear and on to their respective landings to see what all the commotion was about.

Mrs Anderson, emerging from her ground-floor bedroom in dressing-gown and curlers, switched on the hall lights to reveal a dishevelled, frowning, night-gowned Super Gran holding on to the intruder.

'That's funny,' Super Gran murmured, seeing the man clearly for the first time, '*you're* not one of that Inventor's mob, are you?'

'Ow! Ugh! Help! Get 'er off!' the man protested loudly.

'Jings!' the landlady gasped, after she had put on her glasses. 'It's Wilfred! What are *you* doing here? I thought you were down at the Borders, looking for orders?'

'Hey, you down there!' a red-faced English guest on the first-floor landing growled. 'Never mind the Borders – what about *these* boarders? We can't get any sleep because of all this disturbance!'

The guests, assured that it was all a misunderstanding, were coaxed back to their beds. Then Wilfred explained that he had changed his plans and come back to Edinburgh a few days early, and hadn't realized that his room had been given to someone else.

'Wondered why the key wouldn't open the door,' he explained. 'Seemed to be unlocked, but jammed. Didn't know *you* were inside,' he grimaced at Super Gran, as he massaged his many bruises. 'But ...' He suddenly realized that his assailant was a little, white-haired, fragile-looking old lady. And this should have been impossible! 'But . . . you're a . . . little . . .'

'Old lady?' She grinned. 'I'm not, you know. I'm Super Gran!'

He looked her up and down. How could this little old lady have done so much damage to him? 'Felt as if an earthquake, at *least*, had hit me!' he muttered, as he continued to nurse his bruises.

'Come on, son.' Mrs Anderson led the battered, bewildered young man into the lounge. 'You'll just have to sleep the night on the settee. That's all the room I've got left now.'

It took Super Gran about an hour to get back to sleep again. After all the excitement and all the wrestling down two flights of stairs she found that she was all 'go', and it took some time for her heartbeat and her nerves to calm down. She reflected, however, as she drifted off that she had fairly enjoyed the experience, and she wondered if she should have another go at it some time!

It also took Edison some time to settle down again and once more she found herself involved with the Inventor and his mob who, in *this* dream, were chasing her on bicycles while she, naturally, kept having to stop for rests; although the Toughies, surprisingly enough, kept stopping too, to give her a chance!

The faces of Rough and Tough swam into view, scowling down at her in bed, as they demanded: 'Where's that there Super Gran?'

Edison shot up – and stared straight into Rough and Tough's ugly mugs! Right there in her room! Bending over her in bed! About half a metre away! She screamed!

'Super Gran! They're here, they're here! Help!'

As the old lady shot up in bed, her hands karate-ready again, she saw the two Toughies retreating quickly to the door. And if she had stopped to think about it, this might have struck her as being a curious thing for them to do. But she didn't stop to think about it! She merely leapt out of bed and gave chase; out of the door and across the landing to the edge of the stairs.

'Here we go again,' she sighed. 'There's never a dull moment, is there?'

Rough and Tough scrambled down the stairs, two at a time, but Super Gran didn't follow them *that* way. That was too easy! Too ladylike! Too un-Super-Gran-like! She climbed up on to the bannister and zoomed down that instead!

Reaching the first-floor landing she dropped to the floor, ran across it, climbed on to the next sloping hand-rail and zoomed down that too. She arrived at the ground floor and threw herself on top of the Toughies just as *they* reached there, all three of them falling in a heap on the hall floor.

And the noise, once again, brought Edison, Willard, Mrs Anderson, Wilfred and all the other guests (except Mr Black) out of their rooms and on to their landings to see what was going on *this* time!

'Not again!' growled the same annoyed, red-faced boarder; more red-faced than ever! 'Does that woman

84

never stop? Does she spend *all night* attacking people? And what is she, anyway – a retired rugby player? A lady wrestler? A kung fu fighter?' He appealed to whoever would listen to him. 'Can't anyone *do* anything about her? Can't anyone *stop* her? She's a menace, a menace!'

Super Gran, from under the struggling, punching, flailing, biting mass of bodies, heard a 'Pssst! Pssst!' from the open doorway and Rough and Tough, as if by magic, disentangled their limbs from hers, leapt to their feet, scooted out the door and slammed it shut behind them. Then seconds later, while she was scrambling to *her* feet, she heard the sound of a vehicle zooming off with a screech of tyres.

'Now, what was all *that* about?' she murmured, puzzled.

'That's what we *all* want to know!' the grumbler on the landing above her grumbled. 'Do you think we could perhaps all go back to sleep now – or can we expect a *third* performance? Huh? Huh?'

'I *hope* not!' Super Gran muttered, having had – even for her! – enough excitement for *one* night!

As she returned to her room she puzzled over what the episode with the Toughies had been all about. Why had they appeared in her room? Why had they run down the stairs without actually attacking her? Why had they left so suddenly, without trying to kidnap someone – as they always seemed to be doing? There was something wrong, somewhere!

If she hadn't been so tired she would probably have

realized just what they were up to. But it wasn't until the morning that she found out.

Mr Black, who had slept soundly throughout Super Gran's second 'performance', awoke and looked into the corner. And what he *didn't* see there shook him! He looked all round the room; he squinted to see behind Willard's bed; he craned his neck forward to see round the edge of the wardrobe; he looked *every*where; but he didn't see it *any*where. It was gone!

'Willard!' he yelled. 'Wake up! The Shield's gone! It's been stolen!'

But Willard couldn't have cared less right then. He was too tired after all the midnight manoeuvres and he merely moaned musically and turned over in his sleep, ignoring his room-mate.

But someone else heard the man's anguished cry – Super Gran, from two floors away! She wasn't sure if it was her Super-hearing or her mind-reading power, but whatever it was she somehow 'knew' that the Shield had gone – almost as soon as Mr Black knew about it. And despite the fact that she was still asleep at the time!

She jumped out of bed and nudged Edison awake. 'Come on, lassie, wake up. The Shield's gone! From your Dad's room ...'

'Ooooh! Let me sleep!' Edison mumbled, and turned over.

Super Gran thumped a fist into her other palm. 'So *that's* it! It was all a trick to keep me occupied – a diversion – while they pinched the Shield!' The puzzle about the midnight marauders was solved. 'That scunnery Inventor's managed to pinch it after all!'

'Yes, but ...' Edison sleepily inquired as she turned over in bed again, '... what *is* a "scunner", Super Gran?'

The Inventor was proud – not to say surprised – at the success of his scheme to steal the Shield. In fact, it had worked so well that he had to keep pinching himself (which made a change from pinching Shields and Super-machines!) to make sure he wasn't dreaming.

What he had done was this: while Benny and his boys were 'borrowing' a van from a car park, the Inventor had phoned Mrs Anderson, pretending that he was a police officer worried about security.

'You see,' he had explained, 'we've got to know which rooms Super Gran and her friends are occupying. *And* where the Shield is being kept. So we can keep our eyes on them all. You understand?'

'Oh aye, I understand all right,' the old woman had replied – and proceeded to tell him everything he wanted to know. It was as easy as that!

And then, while Rough and Tough had kept Super Gran busy with their wrestling match, Benny had climbed in at the window, crept past the sleeping Mr Black, grabbed the Shield and lowered it out of the window to the waiting Inventor.

'Pssst! Pssst!' The Inventor had then signalled for Rough and Tough to take their leave of Super Gran, and all three of them had dived into the van beside the waiting Benny.

Then Gruff, with his usual 'Ugh!', had driven off with a screech at high speed . . .

9　A(r)rest for the Wicked?

On Tuesday morning a dejected Mr Black set off by
taxi for his conference. He was downcast at having lost
his new wonder invention, which he'd been looking
forward to demonstrating to his fellow inventors.

And Super Gran and the children, who had slept
in after their midnight madness, were equally gloomy
when they eventually emerged from the boarding-house
to wander the city streets aimlessly. They were gloomy
because of the loss of the Shield and aimless because
they didn't know where to start looking for it – or for
the Inventor and his mob.

However, to cheer them up Super Gran suggested
they could do some sightseeing. Which in Edinburgh
isn't difficult – unless you go about with your eyes
closed! For the sights to be seen are all around you.

They walked along Princes Street, with its large,
fashionable shops on one side and its famous Gardens
on the other. They passed the Scott Monument, the
Gardens' huge landmark which dominates the whole
street, and they saw, as a background to the Gardens,
the magnificent Castle on its high peak, which dominates the whole city. And at one o'clock – they heard the
gun!

'Wow!' yelled Edison, almost jumping out of her

socks, as if Tough had crept up behind her and yelled 'Boo!' in her ear!

'Hey! What was that, Gran?' Willard exclaimed. 'It sounded like a gun!'

Super Gran laughed. 'That's probably because it *was* a gun!'

'A gun? You're joking, Super Gran!' Edison couldn't believe it.

'I'm not, you know,' the old lady assured her. 'They fire a gun from the castle every afternoon at one o'clock. To let everyone know that it *is* one o'clock.'

'Hey! Let's go up to the castle, huh, Gran?' Willard suggested.

So they walked uphill over the Mound, the road that cuts through the Gardens from Princes Street, towards the castle high above.

That evening, when they returned to the boarding-house for their meal, they realized that sightseeing was all they had done that day. But the one sight which they hadn't seen was the Inventor and his gang. And they hadn't seen them because the baddies had been having troubles of their own!

The Inventor had changed his plans. Now that he had the Shield he would be able to capture Super Gran, hold her hostage and force Mr Black to make him not only a large supply of Shields, but also a new Super-machine. And even if Super Gran was a match for five men, she certainly was no match for five men plus the Shield!

So they had approached the boarding-house that

morning and stopped the stolen van near by, meaning to pounce on Super Gran when she emerged with Willard and Edison.

However, the Edinburgh police force had other ideas! Instead of the Inventor and company pouncing on Super Gran, the police pounced on the Inventor and company!

'Here they come now. Get ready for a quick grab and getaway,' the Inventor warned Gruff in the driver's seat and the others in the back of the van. 'Benny, you take care of the kids, the rest of us'll shove Super Gran inside the van. Bring the Shield . . .'

Unfortunately, none of them noticed that not only had Gruff stopped the van smack on double yellow lines, where he shouldn't have parked, but he had also stopped it only two feet away from the two feet of a police constable!

And while this was going on, Super Gran and the children were turning the corner beside the boarding-house, unaware of the drama which was about to unfold behind them.

As the Inventor climbed out of the front seat and his gang struggled to clamber out through the back doors of the van with the Shield, the policeman stepped forward.

'Excuse me, sir . . .' The young, gangling constable addressed the Inventor. He had taken one look at the glowering Gruff and decided that the Inventor was the less tough-looking of the two. He was young and in-experienced — but he wasn't daft! 'You're not stopping here, are you?' He pointed to the yellow lines.

'Yes ... er ... no ... er ... ah, well, you see,' spluttered the Inventor, 'we won't be ... ah ... here long, you see ...'

The constable tut-tutted as he ambled leisurely to the front of the van, inspecting it all the way there. He spotted something on the windscreen and slowly proceeded to take a notebook and pencil out of his pocket. Smiling confidently: 'Ah-ha! I see you're not displaying your Vehicle Excise Licence, sir?' He licked his pencil, the way he had seen it done by policemen on the telly. (A bit unhygienic, he thought. But if the telly policemen did it, it *must* be all right, mustn't it? he reckoned.)

'Er ... ah ... no?' said the Inventor, thinking: what's he on about?

'Your Road Fund Licence, sir,' the policeman explained patiently, pointing to the blank windscreen. 'Your disc.'

'Oh ... ah ... yes, of course ... my disc ...' It was just the Inventor's bad luck that his bird-brained crooked companions had snatched a van whose owner – the rotten crook! – was breaking the law.

'*And* you're suffering from baldness too, I see, sir,' the constable continued, politely, but smirking even more confidently. This was his first day out on the beat alone, unsupervised, and he was eager to get some evidence – *any* evidence! – down in his new, unused 'little black book'. And who knows, he thought, maybe it would lead to his very first arrest?

He suddenly glanced round and saw Benny, Rough

and Tough, who had by now managed to emerge from the back of the van with the Shield. He saw the height, weight, breadth and general toughness of them – and he gulped! Maybe this mob was just a wee bit too much for him to tackle, especially on his first day, alone, without help?

'Baldness?' The Inventor brought the policeman's thoughts back to the matter in hand. Panicking, the Inventor put his hand to his head, then sighed with relief on finding that his shock of thick, black hair was intact. 'What baldness? *I'm* not bald!' What was the idiot rabbiting on about, he wondered?

'Tyres, sir, tyres.' The young constable kicked the front near-side one with his size twelves. He didn't quite know *why* people kicked tyres like that, he just knew it was the thing to do! And he edged away from the approaching Toughies at the same time!

'What tires?' the Inventor muttered, misunderstanding. 'Oh, I see! You mean van "tyres" as opposed to – this conversation "tires"! Yes, I see.' He laughed nervously.

By now the policeman was going round examining the other three tyres and was busy scribbling something about each of them in his book.

Hurry up will you you great Scottish nit, the Inventor murmured under his breath, having seen Super Gran and company disappearing round the corner ages ago. Why couldn't the idiot get a move on?

'Let's see, now ...' the constable continued slowly, as if deliberately delaying the Inventor while Super

Gran made her escape. 'No Vehicle Excise Licence, four worn tyres, parking on double yellow lines ...' He bravely went about his business, glancing nervously over his shoulder at the Toughies, who accompanied him – breathing down his neck! – as he went on his tour of inspection.

The Inventor, meanwhile, was cheerfully throttling Gruff for stopping there, and the other Toughies for pinching such a rotten van. But he was doing it only in his imagination – the safest place to do it!

'And one of your number plates is missing ...' The constable took a closer look at the number plate which *wasn't* missing, at the rear of the van, and a frown of remembrance slowly creased his face. He turned to a page at the back of his notebook, he checked the number plate, he checked the notebook again, he looked up at the van itself – at the exhaust smoke which suddenly engulfed him as the vehicle zoomed away from the kerb with a screech of its bald tyres! With Benny, Rough and Tough running after it, throwing the Shield in and scrambling to get aboard before the van reached its top speed!

'Let's get out of here!' the Inventor had yelled to Gruff seconds earlier, achieving one *more* minor ambition – this being another film saying he had always wanted to say!

'Hey! Stop! That van's stolen!' the constable yelled after them, seeing his first 'case', his first arrest, vanishing before his eyes.

He dashed to the nearest passerby and shouted: 'Get

me the polis, Jimmy ... Oh no, I *am* the polis, amn't I?' Then he ran round in a couple of circles looking for a public phone box, before remembering that he was equipped with his very own personal walkie-talkie!

Eventually, after dropping his radio twice in the excitement, he managed to put through a message to headquarters to say that a stolen van had been sighted, heading in the general direction of the Forth Bridges!

So for the rest of the day the Inventor had to forget about trying to capture Super Gran and had to concentrate instead on getting rid of their 'hot' van and replacing it with a new, 'cooler' one!

'And make sure, this time,' he told the Toughies, 'that the owner's not breaking the law – the way that last crook was!'

Mrs Anderson could hardly serve them with their meal that evening, she was so excited. She kept slopping the soup about and dropping chips all over the place in her eagerness to tell them the news.

'They want Super Gran for the British Games,' she informed them, letting a pork sausage fall off a plate on to Willard's knee.

'The British Games?' Super Gran looked up as Willard retrieved the sausage from his dusty knee and ate it.

'Aye, you ken, at Meadowbank. Remember I told you? Well, they want you to run and jump and everything.'

'Hey Gran, that'll be great!' Willard enthused, as he

glanced upwards expectantly, hoping for more sausages to come his way! 'It's not as good as the Olympic Games,' he admitted, 'but this'll be the next best thing.'

'And seeing that they're in Scotland,' Edison chipped in, grinning, 'you *could* say *thistle* be the next best thing!'

Willard and her father stared at her blankly until she explained that the thistle was a Scottish emblem – and that that was meant to be a joke! She shrugged, gave up and went back to her meal.

'And when do they want Super Gran for the Games?' Mr Black asked.

'Tomorrow,' Mrs Anderson told them.

'Tomorrow?'

The old woman turned to Super Gran to explain: 'I was telling a friend about you jumping over walls and everything. And *she* told her brother – one of the officials – who suggested you might like to go there and demonstrate your Super-powers. And tomorrow's the day they're having *other* novelty events, see?'

Super Gran, never one to miss an opportunity to show off, smiled. 'Aye, I must admit I'd love to have a go at breaking some records.'

It might be *bones*, not records, you'll be breaking, Edison thought.

'Havers, lassie!' Super Gran exclaimed in answer to Edison's unspoken thoughts, surprising the others. 'Of course I won't break any bones. Don't be a scaredy-pants all the time!'

'Well, for another thing,' Edison said hesitantly, not

quite daring to say what she was thinking, 'there's the
... ah ... um ...'

'There's the ah um what? Come on, spit it out!'

Edison glanced across the table at her father who,
like Willard, was too busy eating to bother with the
conversation. 'There's ... ah ... um ... Dad's Shield.
We've still to get it back from the Inventor.'

'Och, don't worry, lassie. We'll get it back.'

'Yes, but when? You've got the British Games to go
to now!'

'Och, we can surely have just one wee day off to go
to the Games, can we not?' Super Gran coaxed.

'We-ell ...'

'To show everyone up here how Super I am?' the
old lady went on. 'In my native country?' She frowned.
'They don't seem to have heard of me yet!' She couldn't
understand it. 'And I just want them to see my Super-
speed and my Super-strength, and my Super-eyesight
and my Super-hearing, and my ...'

'All right, all right!' Edison laughed, giving in. 'You
win! By the time you go through the list of your Super-
powers – our food'll be cold!'

10   Fun and Games – at the 'Games'

Next morning Mr Black's taxi dropped off Super Gran and the children at Meadowbank Sports Centre before heading for Leith Town Hall. But the Inventor, who had been lying in wait again with his gang in a 'new' stolen van and had followed the taxi, was puzzled.

'Meadowbank Sports Centre? What on earth are they doing here?' he asked as he watched the crowds going in and the cars queueing up to park.

'Search ... me, boss,' Benny replied. Then he pointed at the posters and banners, reading: 'British Games'.

The Inventor shook his head, still puzzled. 'They're going in to the Games? What's the idea?'

'Ugh?' Gruff asked, gesturing towards the car park entrance.

'Yes,' the Inventor told him, 'we'll park the van.'

But the stadium car park was reserved for vehicles belonging to athletes, officials, the Press and television companies; the public's cars had to be parked a quarter of a mile away, in Holyrood Park – which was too far for the Inventor and his men to walk!

'Drive round to the back of the stadium and find a quiet side-street to park in,' he suggested.

'We need ... money to ... get in, like,' Benny said, holding his hand out, after they had parked the van and walked back to the stadium's main entrance.

The Inventor produced his wallet and examined it. The five train fares to Edinburgh, their 'digs' in the cheapest place they could find, their meals – these had all helped to make a big hole in his bank balance. He was broke! He looked at the admission price, then looked at his wallet again, as if willing it to produce, magically, money which wasn't there!

'Look, Benny . . .' he began, and Benny looked – into his wallet! 'No, I didn't mean: *Look*, Benny, into my wallet! I just meant: Look, Benny – I'm down to my last pound note . . .'

'Huh?'

'The fares,' his boss explained, 'and having to pay for the hotel in advance . . . !' He couldn't understand why people, seeing him with four obvious crooks, demanded their money before supplying the goods! 'And you *will* all eat big meals, too . . .' he complained, quietly.

He didn't want to complain *too* much as he didn't relish being lifted up by the throat again! It still hurt when he thought about it!

'Benny, I'm broke.' He lowered his voice. 'Couldn't you . . . ah . . . *do* something about it?' Benny looked blank, as usual. '*You* know.' The Inventor nudged him and winked, trying to make the baddie take the hint without actually telling him to break the law.

'Oh!' At last, Benny understood. His face brightened. Light dawned. 'Sure, boss . . . sure . . .'

He slipped in amongst the crowds gathering near the

turnstiles and returned, a few minutes later, with a fistful of fivers. 'Will this . . . do, like . . . ?' he grinned.

'Well, it'll do to be going on with,' the Inventor admitted.

They paid their admission money at the turnstile boxes, passed through the concourse, where dozens of kiosks and stalls were selling programmes, souvenirs, sweets, drinks and crisps, and went up into the main stadium, where most of the sports events would be taking place.

After they had been inside for half an hour and the first heats of the track events had taken place, the Inventor became restless. He was bored. He didn't particularly like athletics meetings and he was wondering what they were all doing there in the first place. He turned to Benny. 'Come on, there's nothing happening here. Let's go . . .'

Suddenly, as he turned to leave, there was an announcement over the loudspeaker that there were to be three extra, unscheduled, novelty events taking place that day.

'First of all,' the announcer said, 'there will be a demonstration of athletic feats with, who knows, some records broken by . . . wait for it . . . a little old lady who calls herself Super Gran! Ha ha!' He obviously didn't believe it was possible!

The Inventor turned back, pricking up his ears at this. 'Ah-ha! So *that's* what she's here for, is it?'

'Secondly,' the announcement continued, 'the Air

Force Flyers will be demonstrating their prowess on the trampoline. And thirdly, like many Scottish towns and villages, we shall be holding our very own Mini Highland Games. With caber-tossing, throwing the hammer, tug-o'-war and' – he paused for effect – 'a "hurling the haggis" competition!'

'Did you hear that, Benny?' the Inventor murmured to his henchman.

'Yeah, boss . . . an 'aggis . . . 'urlin' compet –'

'I DON'T LIKE 'AGGIS!' Tough interrupted, bawling as usual.

'Oh, ye don't, don't ye, Jimmy?' A huge, hairy, bearded, kilted Scotsman, built like a tartan tank, glared at Tough, eyeball to eyeball, daring him to continue insulting his national dish.

'No I DON'T!' Tough glared back, inviting a fight.

'I didn't mean the *haggis*,' the Inventor cut in, nudging Benny, hoping that he would stop Tough and the hairy Scot coming to blows. 'I meant the first thing – Super Gran's demonstration.'

'Oh yeah . . . that?' Benny nodded as he prised the two tough guys apart.

'Listen, Benny, I've got an idea. I'm going to give that show-off a showing-up. Super Gran, I mean.'

'Wot you . . . gonna do . . . like?' Benny asked.

'I'm gonna get the . . . I mean, I'm *going* to get the Shield out of the van – to challenge Super Gran to do her tricks through it.'

'Yeah?'

'Yeah . . . I mean, *yes*. But of course, she'll fail . . .'

'Of . . . course,' Benny agreed but stood silent, looking puzzled. 'But . . . why . . . ?'

'Because she *can't* do her Super-tricks when the Shield's near her. And she'll be made to look a right fool, too. *And* in front of this big crowd!' He laughed as he gestured all round.

Benny shrugged and turned his attention to the 400 metres hurdles, taking place right then.

'I'm going to fetch the Shield from the van,' the Inventor went on. He nodded towards Gruff. 'You come and help me carry it.'

'Ugh!' the one-word Toughie complained. He was just beginning to get interested in the athletic proceedings.

'You, Benny, and . . .' – the Inventor nodded towards Rough and Tough – 'wait here for us. By the way, Benny . . .' He turned back, before following Gruff through the crowd. 'What *are* their names? The Toughies . . . er, I mean – your boys?'

'Well . . . now, ah . . . that one . . . there is . . .'

The Inventor didn't wait. 'Don't bother, Benny. You can tell me afterwards!' He was off, following in the wake of the muscular Gruff who was elbowing a passageway through the crowd behind them. By the time the slow-speaking Benny told the inventor the Toughies' real names – the Games would be long over!

Benny, however, was just having his good idea. His GREAT IDEA! And as it slowly filtered into his mind he decided to put it into operation right away.

So the Inventor was short of cash? Then why shouldn't he and his boys help him out, Benny thought? Why shouldn't they obtain some money now? Right here and now? Why wait to return to the city centre to knock off a shop or a bank? Why not pull the job here? At the stadium? Why not take the takings from the box office?

'Come on ... lads,' he muttered, as he led them out of the crowd. 'I've gotta ... great idea ... like. It's ... like this ...'

First of all, each of them 'borrowed' a tracksuit from one of the athletes' changing-rooms when the security guard was having his tea-break. Then, after being refused admission to the administrative area without an official pass card, each of them 'borrowed' a pass from a passing athlete to get through.

Suitably 'disguised' as athletes, they made their way to the offices, intending to rob the safe, stuff their ill-gotten gains inside the tracksuits – and scarper. For the tracksuits would hold hundreds – maybe even thousands? – of pounds. It was a great idea! Why hadn't someone thought of it before?

The cashier looked up from sorting used tickets into bundles to see three large, broken-nosed, flat-eared, tough-looking men in tracksuits glaring down at him.

'Come on ... 'and it ... over, like ...' Benny commanded, in his toughest, most threatening voice. Which was an offer that the cashier couldn't refuse!

'Wh-what, th-these? H-here you are ...' The man,

puzzled, handed over a bundle of tickets, which Rough roughly grabbed from him.

'What? These're no use, it's *money* we're after,' Rough rasped, tossing the bundle back down on the desk.

'B-but – we don't have m-much m-money h-here,' the terrified cashier stammered. 'Most people s-sent in their m-money and bought their t-tickets m-months ago! We've only got the h-handed-in tickets h-here!'

'Huh?' said Benny.

'WHADDA WE DO NOW?' Tough yelled, deafening the cashier who was now being tied up and gagged by Rough.

'I . . . dunno, like . . .' Benny confessed.

Just then a security guard entered, carrying a large leather bag in each hand. 'Hi, Joe! Here are the takings from the souvenir stalls to put in your safe . . . Huh . . . ?' he said, before he too was pounced on to be tied up and gagged.

'That's somethin'!' Rough muttered grudgingly as he grabbed the bags. He hauled the banknotes out and stuffed them inside his tracksuit. 'Better than nothin'.'

Benny and Tough did the same, giving their victims cause to wonder briefly how these 'athletes' were going to be able to run or jump with tracksuits full of money!

So Benny's plan worked – to begin with. And it might have continued to work if Tough, like the other two, had been content to take bank*notes*. But Benny and Rough didn't discover this until later! And that was their *first* mistake.

Their second mistake was in turning the wrong way when they left the cashier's office.

They had intended to jog quietly to the office-block exit a few metres away, escape outside, and park their loot in their parked van. (Then they'd remove the track-suits, which would fool pursuing police who'd be looking for athletes as the culprits!) But instead, by mistake, they jogged the opposite way: back down the stairs, along a corridor, through the crowded concourse, into the stadium – and on to the running-track!

Meanwhile, as the RAF gymnasts positioned their trampoline on the grass in the centre of the track, Super Gran had been showing off her Super-powers to the crowd.

She had competed in – and easily won! – the 100 metres sprint, zooming past all the other top-class competitors. Then, as most of them claimed that they hadn't really been trying against a little old lady, she raced them in the 200 metres – in which they really *were* trying. And once again she zoomed past them, to their annoyance!

'I wouldn't mind having a go at yon trampoline thing,' she murmured, eyeing it. 'But I'm going to try the long jump, the high jump and the triple jump first.'

'What's the triple jump, Super Gran?' Edison asked.

'It's like the hop, step and jump, idiot!' Willard cut in scathingly.

Super Gran then out-threw the country's leading javelin-throwers, much to *their* annoyance; and the discus-throwers, much to *their* annoyance. And then it was time for her to try the pole vaulting.

'But they don't even *allow* women to do pole vaulting,' Willard exclaimed. 'Only the men.'

'Havers!' the liberated little old lady snorted. 'I'm as good as a man, *any* day! And besides,' she joked, 'I don't *want* to vault over a gentleman from Poland!'

As she had never seen a vaulting-pole before (apart from on television, of course), she had to have instruction in using one. How to hold it, how to run up to the jumping-off point with it, how to clear the crossbar, how – and when – to let go of the pole, and how to land on the large foam-rubber landing mattress.

She carried the pole back about two dozen paces and then, while the crowd held its communal breath, she ran forward to the jumping-off point. As she ran she pointed the front end of the pole towards the box on the ground at the foot of the uprights and then, with the pole bending backwards, she rose into the air. Up she went and over the crossbar.

Then she continued to rise, higher and higher, beating the other contestants. Then she beat the British record, then the European record, the Commonwealth, the World and finally the Olympic record!

She had remembered to drop the pole at the right time as she soared upwards. But the trouble was, the jump had taken her too high! And what goes up must come down! And on the way down, if she missed the

mattress – she would break every bone in her little old body.

But, on the other hand, if she *hit* the mattress – where would she land . . . ?

11 · Caber Capers!

Super Gran, kicking her legs furiously in the air as if riding an invisible bicycle, came zooming down to earth, landing, luckily, on the mattress. But then she bounced forward and upward on it, yelling: 'Ye-ow!'

She whizzed through the air towards the RAF's trampoline, from which the Air Force Flyers flew in all directions – to avoid being hit by a UFO (an Unforgettable Flying Oldie, as Super Gran had once before referred to herself).

She bounced from the trampoline, forward again, towards the high jump uprights and the mattress behind it. She cleared the crossbar, landed on the mattress and bounced for the third time, each bounce being lower and slower than the previous one, until she cleared the long jump and landed, finally, in the sand-pit behind it, narrowly missing a jealous jumper and two fearful officials!

While the crowd slowly exhaled its painfully held breath and began to clap and cheer, Willard and Edison ran towards her to see if she had broken any bones.

'Broken any bones?' She indignantly brushed the sand off herself. 'Broken any *records* is more like it!'

She stood up, did a little curtsey to the cheering, applauding spectators and said: 'That'll save me trying the high jump, the long jump, the triple jump *and* the trampoline!' She grinned cheekily. 'Although I could always have *another* go at them!'

'Well *I* don't think you *should* have another go,' Edison said, as her face resumed its normal shade, having been white with fright at Super Gran's antics. 'Don't try anything as dangerous again.'

'Blethers, lassie! It was just like flying!' She laughed. 'And there was me saying a couple of days ago that I couldn't fly!'

'I wish *I* could've tried that,' Willard said enviously. His Gran had *all* the fun. He just wished that *he* were like Super Gran. If only she had made *him* Super when she'd had the chance, before the Super-machine had blown up.

Super Gran looked all around to see what else she could have a go at. 'What's next?' she asked eagerly.

'Haven't you tried enough things, Super Gran?' Edison said worriedly. She didn't want the old lady to push her luck too far.

'What? You're joking! There's plenty more things for me to try.'

'Yeah! And you've been beatin' all these superstar athletes, Gran,' Willard beamed. '*And* the records.'

'I'm a bit of a superstar myself,' Super Gran boasted. 'I can just see my name up in lights: "Super Gran, Superstar"!'

'Yes, and you're giving all these superstar athletes a proper showing up too,' Edison quietly scolded her. 'They won't be too pleased with you.'

The old lady's day-dream bubble burst. 'You know, lassie, you're quite right. I never thought of that. I should be ashamed of myself.'

'We-ell . . .'

'No, you're right. It's *not* fair, is it? It's only right that *they* should get the limelight,' the old lady conceded. Although the limelight was what she herself craved, now that she was Super. 'Tell you what, I'll try just one more thing, eh?'

She couldn't resist it. Nor could she resist being the centre of attraction and showing off. After all, she thought, after about seventy years of *not* being the centre of attraction, what harm could there be in a *wee* bit of showing off?

She looked round again and spotted a dozen haggises lying on a table and a caber lying on the grass, waiting to be tossed. 'Ah! The caber!' she exclaimed. 'I've always wanted to toss the caber!'

'The caber!' Edison almost had a tartan fit when she saw what her old friend was proposing to toss – a tree-trunk, the length of a telegraph pole! 'That's far too heavy for you! You couldn't even *lift* it, never mind toss it anywhere!'

'Who couldn't? Have I got to remind you, lassie, that I'm Super Gran and that I can do . . .'

'*Any*thing – yes, I know,' Edison sighed. 'But I mean – tossing the caber . . . ?' That was just *too* much! Even for Super Gran!

The little old lady went over and lifted it. Just like that! She held it upright in her arms, then she ran forward a few paces and tossed it. It went zooming up into the air, turned over and came whizzing back down again, making a large dent in the turf.

She ran over and picked it up once more. To have another go.

'Super Gran!' Edison admonished. 'You said *one* more go at something, that was all. You promised.'

'Och, wheesht, lassie. I'm just *going* to have one more go!' She giggled. She could keep saying that all day!

It was just at that moment that Benny and his wandering warriors appeared in the stadium. They jogged in their bulging tracksuits across the running-track and on to the grass, but the jogging had a jingle-jangle sound to it.

Realizing that they had jogged the wrong way, Benny stopped – and Rough bumped into him! Then Tough bumped into Rough – with the sound of an extra-loud jangle!

'We've come ... the wrong ... way, like,' Benny muttered. 'Ouch!'

'Ow!' Rough barked.

'Oh!' Tough bawled.

'Shhh!' Benny warned, turning on them. 'An' wot's ... that noise?'

'Wot noise?' asked Rough.

'That there ... janglin' noise ... ?'

'Dunno!' Rough shrugged. '*I* don't hear no janglin' noise.'

'NOR ME NEITHER!' roared Tough.

'Not now ... like, it's ... stopped,' Benny told them.

114

'Never mind that,' Rough said. 'Where'll we go? Everyone's lookin' at us. We've been rumbled!'

'Don't panic ... like,' Benny commanded out of the corner of his mouth. 'Act noncher ... nonchal ... non-cha-long ... er ... ah ... stay cool, man! Go back ... the way ... we came ... like ...'

'NO, GO FORWARD!' Tough suggested, at the top of his voice as usual.

They collided again, and again there came the loud jingle-jangle noise. Then they decided that the best thing would be for them to continue across the grass to the other side of the stadium and try to slip in amongst the crowd.

'Walk!' ordered Benny, at the front of the tiptoeing threesome. 'Then no ... one'll notice ... us, like ...'

But even just tiptoeing slowly across the grass some-how produced the usual strange jingle-jangle sound.

'There it is ... again,' a puzzled Benny muttered over his shoulder to Rough behind him. 'That there ... janglin' noise ... hear it?'

'Yeah! Wot is it?' Rough roughly asked Tough, over *his* shoulder.

'I DUNNO!' Tough, bringing up the rear, shrugged *his* shoulders – and the jangling sound increased more than somewhat!

Super Gran, who had been poised to toss the caber for the second time, saw the three tracksuited figures at the far end of the field, jogging slowly along in single file with, even at *that* distance, a slight jangling sound.

'Here!' she murmured softly. 'There's something just a wee bit familiar about yon three fat athletes!'

'What do you mean, Gran?'

'It's just a feeling I've got, laddie. They look to me like ...'

'The Toughies?' Edison gasped.

Super Gran nodded. 'I wonder what *they're* up to?' She zoomed in her Super-sight and tuned in her Super-hearing in time to hear Rough saying:

'It's *him*, Benny. That li'l idiot! 'E filled 'is tracksuit with coins! No wonder there's been a janglin' noise all the time. It's *him* rattlin'!'

'Oh ... no,' Benny muttered. 'The silly ... sickener! Didn't we ... say to ... snatch just ... banknotes ... not coins ... you clot ...?'

'YOU DID NOT!' Tough yelled back along the line. 'NO ONE NEVER SAID NOTHIN' 'BOUT NO COINS, NO WAY!'

'Ah-ha!' exclaimed Super Gran in triumph, hardly needing her Super-hearing where Tough was concerned. 'So that's it, is it?'

'It's that scunnersome Inventor's hoodlum horrors,' she explained. 'And they've just robbed the stadium, by the looks of it.'

She dropped the caber to the ground (at which the crowd, thinking it was an accident, gasped in consternation). Then she lifted it again, but this time held it lengthwise in her arms, parallel to the ground (at which the crowd gasped in admiration). She ran a few metres with it and threw it – at the three

Toughies (at which the crowd gasped in anticipation)!

The caber flew through the air, hit the ground a dozen metres from the tiptoeing Toughies and rolled towards them at Super-speed.

Benny looked sideways, saw the careering caber coming and warned his men – but of course Benny spoke too slowly! 'Look ... out!' he yelled. But he'd only got the 'out' out when the caber mowed them down and burst their tracksuits open, causing coins to cascade and fivers to flutter all over the grass!

By this time the tied and gagged cashier and security guard had been freed, and an announcement was made for the rest of the security staff to apprehend three criminals, disguised as athletes, who had robbed the office.

While some officials and competitors scrambled about retrieving the paper money which was blowing about in the breeze, Super Gran, seeing the Toughies struggling to their feet, looked round for something else to throw at them. She grabbed a haggis in each hand from the table on which they lay – and pelted Benny and company with them! Then she grabbed another two and pelted them again, and again!

The Toughies, forgetting their loot in their eagerness to dodge the milling officials and the Super-flung haggises, ran towards the crowd at the rear of the stadium, seeking escape.

Super Gran tried to pursue and capture them – but she never got there! For she was soon surrounded by a crowd of admirers, all eager to slap her back and

shake her hand, to congratulate her not only on her athletic prowess but also on her thief-catching abilities. (Even though she hadn't actually caught them!)

The old lady shrugged and resigned herself to the adulation of her new fans. The Toughies would just have to escape – this time. It couldn't be helped.

Meanwhile, the Inventor had also been having his troubles.

He and Gruff had collected the Shield from the van, as planned, but the bother began when they tried to get back in through the turnstiles at the rear of the stadium. They had thrown away their tickets and the turnstile man was demanding payment from them once again. Which irked the thrifty Inventor, who resented having to pay for something twice and who argued for fifteen minutes with the man before finally paying up.

Then, after all that, they discovered that the Shield was too big to get in through the turnstile anyway! So they had paid their money – twice – for nothing! Which irked the Inventor even more!

However, the Inventor, not to be beaten, was in the process of endeavouring, somehow, to get the Shield through – when Benny and the others came running out towards him. He and Gruff had been pushing, pulling, thrusting and shoving the Shield, but now the Inventor stopped as Benny called to him:

'Hey ... boss, run ... for it ... like ...'

'Benny? What ... ? What's wrong?' The Inventor

looked from the still struggling Gruff to the rapidly approaching Toughies.

What were they running for? Why were they leaving? Weren't they going to help Gruff with the Shield? Weren't they going to help *him* give Super Gran a showing up? Why did they look so battle-scarred? Why were they dressed in torn tracksuits? Why tracksuits? Where did *they* get tracksuits?

'Run for it!' Rough repeated raspingly. He tried to leap over one of the turnstiles, but it was a boxed-in one, with a roof – which he attempted to demolish with his head! 'Ow! Ouch!' he cried.

'But ... !' The Inventor stood still, looking more puzzled than ever. 'But, Benny ... ?'

'RUN FOR IT, YOU DOZY DOPE!' Tough thundered at him.

'But ... what are you doing out here? Where are you going? I've got *plans* for you ...' he protested feebly. 'And we paid *twice* to get in, too!' He almost wept.

'Run!' Rough repeated, rubbing his clattered cranium. 'We're rumbled!' He struggled out past the turnstile, followed by Tough and Benny.

Then Gruff, realizing that something was wrong, dropped the Shield and took to his heels behind them, and the four of them sped to the side-street where the van was parked.

'What's going on?' The Inventor slowly picked up the Shield and slowly went to follow his retreating ruffians.

He picked up speed only when he looked back over his shoulder and saw six sturdy security men bearing down on him ...

'He-elp! Wait for me!' he yelled to his men as he ran.

12 Goings-on in the Gardens

The next morning the Inventor and his mob were sitting, all crushed up together, on a seat in Princes Street Gardens. They had intended making another kidnap attempt on Super Gran, but Rough, Tough and Benny's caber-clobbered bodies were so sore that they'd taken ages to climb out of their beds and were too late!

'Look! Look at this!' exclaimed the Inventor suddenly, pointing to the 'What's On in Edinburgh Today' column of his newspaper.

'Wot ... is it ... boss?' Benny asked as he nursed his bruises.

'It's that confounded Super Gran again!'

He had already seen the paper's action photos from the Games, including one of her with a haggis in each hand, harassing his hapless hoodlums. And he had muttered curses about her and the publicity she was getting.

'Wot is it this time?' Rough inquired, as he and Tough leaned towards the paper from one side while Benny and Gruff leaned across from the other side – flattening the Inventor in the process!

He tried to move his arms, now pinned against his

sides, to make himself more room – but couldn't. 'She's
... ouch ... giving another ... ow ... demonstration.
Here ... ouch ... in the Gardens ... ow ... this morning ...'

'WOT KINDA DEMONSTRATION?' Tough bawled.
'NOT TOSSIN' 'AGGISES, I 'OPE! I 'ATE 'AGGISES!'

Do you mean you 'ate' them or you 'hate' them, the
Inventor wondered. But he thought better about
wondering out loud!

The Inventor's face broke into a smile quicker than
the Toughies could have broken into a bank! 'Never
mind that. Don't you see? She's coming *here* – at half-
past eleven. So that's our chance to nab her – without
having to look for her!'

'Well, I 'ope she 'asn't got 'aggises with 'er!' Rough
rumbled, as he idly, and without thinking about it,
squashed flat the metal waste-paper basket which stood
near the seat – just for practice!

But something was bothering Benny. 'Boss ... why
do ... you wanna ... nab 'er? You've got ... the Shield
... 'aven't you ... like?'

The Inventor put his paper down to count off the
reasons on his fingers. 'I've told you before – I want
to hold her hostage, to make Black work for me.
Secondly: I want to use the Shield against her, to give
her a showing up – for showing off! Thirdly: I want
to get my own back on her for that Super-machine
business, where *she* ended up Super and *we* didn't. And
fourthly: I just want to get her, d'you hear? To get
her, d'you hear? To get her, d'you ...'

'HERE!' Tough yelled, grabbing the Inventor by the collar and partly throttling him, to stop him going all hysterical. 'WATCH IT!'

Once the Inventor had calmed down and Tough had released him, he continued: 'So that's it settled? We'll fetch the Shield along here and we'll make her Super-less long enough for you four to grab her, shove her into the van, tie her up with ropes, and ...'

'Ropes?' Benny shrugged. 'Where do ... we get ... ropes round ... 'ere, like?'

'You can pinch some out of the gardeners' huts, or somewhere,' the Inventor suggested. 'Now, this is what we'll do ...'

Benny and Gruff went off to fetch the Shield from the van and ropes from the huts. While the Inventor, rubbing his hands together at the thought of capturing Super Gran at last, left the Gardens with Rough and Tough – to go shopping for a wig! Or rather, to go shop-*lifting* with Rough and Tough!

An Edinburgh Council official had seen Super Gran performing at the Games and thought it would add a touch of variety to the bands, dancers and pop groups which entertained in the Gardens if the old lady demonstrated her Super-powers there.

'Is tomorrow the last day of your Dad's conference?' Super Gran asked Edison as she and the children made their way through the Gardens towards the stage.

The girl nodded glumly. 'And he's disappointed at not having the Shield to show them. I don't think they believed him when he told them about it. *And* we still haven't got it back yet,' she added bitterly.

'Och, don't worry,' Super Gran said cheerily. 'We'll go and look for that scunnery Inventor – just as soon as I've finished my performance here. I promise you.'

They reached the stage and were met by the small, chubby compère who would introduce her to the audience. 'Ah, there you are ... ah ... Super Gran, is it?' He gave a little nervous laugh, and sniffed.

Super Gran nodded. 'That's right, laddie. That's me – Super Gran.'

'Ah, good. Good.' He looked at his watch. 'Well, if you're ready ... ?' he said as he stepped forward to the microphone to introduce her to the audience.

For the next half-hour the old lady went through her paces on the stage and on the grass near by. She demonstrated her Super-eyesight and hearing; she lifted large, heavy men above her head; she zoomed back and forward across a couple of hundred metres of grass at high speed; she tore in half a telephone directory (which a young man had brought with him in the hope of foiling her!) – afterwards throwing the two halves aside without thinking.

A little white poodle, sniffing about on the grass, saw the large pieces of directory whizzing towards it and didn't stop to argue. It took to its heels!

'Oops! Sorry, wee poodle!' Super Gran apologized. 'It's nothing personal!'

Then she whistled for the dog to come back – to

forgive and forget! – but forgot that her whistle was a Super-whistle! And not only was the poodle deafened, everyone in the Gardens was deafened as well!

What's that little old lady got against me? the poodle wondered in its doggy way, as it took to its heels once again!

Super Gran positively beamed, loving every minute of her performance and lapping up the crowd's applause.

Then, suddenly, while doing her mind-reading act as a breather between the more strenuous feats, she got a shock.

'You've recently returned from Canada,' she had been telling a large woman.

'Yes, you're right,' the woman agreed. 'Toronto, on holiday.'

Super Gran's attention wandered away from the woman – she was getting the distinct impression that the Inventor was in the audience somewhere. In disguise. But she could detect his thoughts, which went something like this:

'Get her ... this time ... sure! Won't ... suspect anything! Challenge her ... carry me round ... back of stage ... Toughies grab ... give her ... showing up ... with Shield ... she'll be ... helpless. Hold her ... hostage ... Black ... Super-machine ...'

Super Gran thought quickly. She didn't want to face the Shield against which she was powerless – not to mention the four Toughies. She'd be hopelessly out-numbered. There was nothing else for it, much as it hurt her pride – she would have to make a run for it again (as she had done before in London, from Roly's mob).

Anyway, she thought, it was better to run away and 'live to fight another day' – on *her* terms, rather than on the Inventor's. But she would have to do it craftily and not appear to be a coward.

'Now for my next wee trick ...' she announced, turning to the children. 'Willie, Edison, come over here, will you?' She addressed the audience again, and joked: 'For this feat – I need the children's feet!'

She bent down and put her hands on the grass, palms upwards. Then she asked the children to stand on them, one on each hand. 'Are you ready? I'm going to lift you.'

'You're what, Super Gran?' Edison's screech was full of panic! 'You're joking!'

'Wheeesht, lassie! Trust me!' the old lady whispered.

She straightened up and lifted the children into the air, until they were level with her elbows. Slowly she started to trot with them towards the trees, *away* from her audience. Regretfully! For Super Gran was always reluctant to leave an audience!

'Hey! What's the idea, Gran?' Willard grinned, enjoying the ride.

When she had safely trotted a few hundred metres along a footpath behind some trees which hid them from the audience (and from the Inventor), she told the children to sit on her shoulders, one on each side, and she speeded up a bit.

'Oh! Oh! Careful, Super Gran!' Edison cried, clutching at the little old lady's head to keep from falling, and knocking Super Gran's tartan tammy over her eyes in doing so.

Meanwhile the Inventor, disguised in a carrot-red wig and a black, droopy, Mexican moustache, was patiently awaiting, with the audience, Super Gran's return – not realizing that she had fooled him again!

'But what are we running for?' Edison asked, when she had recovered her balance, and her courage, and was beginning to enjoy being zoomed along the narrow path, zigzagging around astonished passersby.

Super Gran dashed along to the end of that part of the Gardens and turned right to run across a bridge over the railway line. 'It was an ambush,' she explained, 'or at least it *would've* been if I hadn't read the Inventor's mind back there.'

She panted up a zigzag slope and then up some steps to street-level, at the Mound, going uphill towards the castle. She slowed down a bit.

'The Inventor?' Willard gasped. '*I* didn't see the Inventor!'

'Neither did I,' admitted Edison.

'He was disguised again,' Super Gran told them. 'In a silly red wig and a daft droopy moustache!'

'Was *that* the Inventor?' Edison said, amazed. 'I didn't realize.'

'*And* his gang were waiting behind the stage to waylay me with the Shield!'

'Oh no, Super Gran!'

'Oh yes, lassie! But don't worry, we're safe now.'

While she was trotting slowly up the Mound with the children sitting on her shoulders, two middle-aged women shoppers passed, going down into Princes Street.

'Disgraceful!' one of them snapped. 'Big lumps like that expecting a little old lady to carry *them* about! Disgusting!'

'Yes, awful, isn't it?' her friend agreed as they both stopped to glare at the selfish, callous children. 'It's more like *them* carrying *her* about!'

Edison flushed, embarrassed. 'Yes, Super Gran, put us down now. We'll walk. You've carried us far enough.'

'Havers, lassie! I could carry you for miles. Nae bother!'

'Yeah,' Willard agreed. 'Belt up, Red! I *like* bein' carried!'

'Yes, *you* would,' Edison retorted. '*All* babies like being carried!'

'Hey! *I'm* not a baby!'

'Yes you are!'

'Here! That's enough!' Super Gran dropped them to the ground before they came to blows above her head!

They turned into Ramsay Lane, a short, steep, cobbled roadway which led towards the castle on the hill.

'Will the Inventor come after us?' asked Edison worriedly.

'Maybe he's rounded up his gang by now,' Willard suggested, glancing back down the lane. 'Maybe they're just behind us . . . !'

'*Are* they coming after us, Super Gran?' Edison was

really worried now. 'Can't you tell, with your Super-powers?'

'I can't see or hear *that* far away!' She shook her head, but smiled. 'I know I'm good, but even Super Gran's not *that* goo –'

She suddenly stopped – talking *and* walking. She was looking up at a notice on the building they had reached at the top of the lane, just round the corner from the castle esplanade. It read: 'Outlook Tower. Camera Obscura. Scottish crafts. Books. Records.' She looked thoughtful. 'But I know how we can find out.' She pointed to the Tower's entrance. 'In here!'

'Here?' The children looked puzzled.

She nodded. 'I remember this place from years ago.' She took her tartan purse out of her cardigan pocket and fished out the entrance money. 'It's a Camera Obscura, you see.'

'A what?' said Willard, puzzled. 'An obscure camera?'

'A Camera Obscura,' Edison corrected him scornfully, pointing at another notice near the doorway. 'Can't you read, Willie?'

''Course I can! And don't call me "Willie", Red!'

'Well don't call me "Red", Willie . . .'

'The Camera Obscura,' Super Gran cut in, as she held them apart, like a wrestling referee caught between two glaring, growling grapplers on Saturday afternoon TV, 'is a gadget that's going to help us see where the Inventor and his mob are. Come on, let's go in . . .'

13 Does the Camera Obscura Pickpocket?

'But what *is* it?' Willard insisted, as they joined the queue for tickets.

'It's something they used to have in the old days,' his Gran explained. 'It works with mirrors and a . . . a sort of periscope thing, I think.'

'Yes, but what does it *do*, Gran?' Willard persisted.

'It shows you a picture of Edinburgh. On a white table, if I remember rightly. The light shines down from the mirrors at the top of the Tower on to the table, and you stand and look down at it.'

'Something like television?' Edison suggested.

'Aye, but they had this long before the telly was invented,' she said, as the queue moved forward. 'I used to think it was great, before we had the telly, seeing the people walking about and the traffic moving, just as it was actually happening.'

They reached the pay-desk, handed over their money and then moved towards the Tower steps – where a sudden thought struck Edison:

'Crumbs! How many steps are there?' The idea of climbing a tower didn't exactly fill her with joy!

'There – are – ninety – eight – steps – to – the –

Tower,' Willard cheerfully announced, reading it word for word from a notice on the wall.

'What?' Edison, already out of breath after climbing eight steps, was shaken!

'Och! Ninety-eight steps? That's nothing!' Super Gran exclaimed. 'You take your time. Take a wee rest now and then if you like. I'll race young Willie here to the top! How's that?'

'Righto, Gran, you're on!' Willard eagerly accepted the challenge.

Edison was content to climb the Tower slowly at her own pace, stopping every few minutes to rest and look at the photographs of 'Old Edinburgh' which adorned the walls. And she was content to see Willard and his Gran (taking two at a time!) go zooming up the steps ahead of her.

The little old lady and her grandson whizzed up and around the bends in the stairway, colliding occasionally with the other Camera-viewers; those going up *and* those coming down from the previous performance.

'What's that, Gran?' Willard asked, as they shot past the second-floor landing.

'Looks like an exhibition,' Super Gran replied. 'Never mind, we'll see it on our way down.'

They reached the top landing, which also served as a waiting-room (Super Gran having let Willard win the race, to please him!), to find over a dozen people waiting there for the next 'show' to start.

There were two women, a bald-headed man and a couple of teenagers, as well as small groups of foreigners

– Germans, Italians and Americans – chatting amongst themselves.

'We've got five minutes to wait yet,' a man told them as he looked at his watch.

'Five minutes, is that all?' Super Gran looked towards the stairway to see if Edison was coming, but knowing really that she wouldn't be for a long time yet. 'Will the lassie get here in time?'

'Huh!' Willard snorted. 'She'll be *hours* yet.'

'I'd better go down and bring her up,' Super Gran decided, as more people arrived at the waiting-room.

'And I'm goin' to see what's out here,' said Willard, heading for the outside balcony, which gave a good view of the city below.

Super Gran ran down the stairs – dodging the people who kept getting in her way! – and almost collided with a man coming up, whose appearance was striking, to say the least!

He had a small *white* beard and *reddish* bushy eye-brows and he wore a *purple* suit, *pink* cowboy boots and a *green* velvet cap!

When Super Gran reached Edison – who was only a quarter of the way up! – she found the girl taking a rest. Naturally!

'How about taking a lift?' the old lady suggested.

'A lift?' Edison looked round, puzzled. 'I didn't know there *was* a lift. I thought there was just these stairs?'

Super Gran laughed. 'I meant: how about taking a lift from *me*?' She yanked the girl off her feet and, despite

Edison's protests and embarrassment, ran back up the stairs again – carrying her!

'Super Gran! Put me down! That's *twice* now you've carried me!'

But the little old lady just ignored her.

'Super Gran! Did you see *him*!' Edison whispered, as they overtook the peculiarly dressed man near the top of the stairs.

'I couldn't *help* seeing him!' Super Gran giggled.

'Nothing matches. He's a multicoloured odd-bod!' Edison said.

'And you'll see a few like him in Edinburgh,' Super Gran smiled, as they reached the waiting-room and she put an embarrassed, blushing Edison down. 'Especially when the Edinburgh Festival's on!'

While the old lady went to fetch Willard in from the balcony, the Camera's viewing-room doors opened, the first-show viewers emerged and the next show's viewers started to enter. And while all this mingling was going on, something happened which made Edison gasp.

'Hey, Super Gran!' she whispered urgently, as Willard and his Gran stepped in from the balcony. 'He's a thief!'

'Who is?'

'The odd-bod! He put his hand into that bald man's pocket!'

'Wow! A pickpocket!' exclaimed Willard.

'What'll we do, Super Gran?'

'Do?' She was astonished at the girl's question. 'Do? We catch him, what else?'

But before any of them could do anything they realized that most of the people in the waiting-room had shuffled their way up the four steps into the small, dusky viewing-room.

'Where's he got to?' Edison looked round the emptying room, but the man was nowhere in sight.

'He must be inside with the others,' Super Gran suggested. 'Come on, let's go in.'

'Walk right round please, right round,' the guide instructed them, as he ushered about twenty viewers into the room, the first ones taking their places round a white, circular table in the room's centre, while the others climbed three steps to a little gallery. Then, as Super Gran and the children entered, last of all, the guide closed the door and switched off the room's one light, leaving a few dull red ones on.

'Which one's the pickpocket?' Willard demanded, in a voice of which even Tough would have been proud! The other viewers turned and glared at him in the gloom.

'Shush!'

'Wheeesht! Not so loud!' his Gran warned him.

'Super Gran!' Edison gasped, as her eyes got used to the dimness and she looked round the room. 'He's not here!'

'Then where's the wee bachle got to?'

'He must've slipped down the stairs with the last crowd going out. He hasn't come in!' Edison said.

Super Gran turned towards the door, as if to rush after the pickpocket, but hesitated.

'And there's the man he robbed,' Edison went on in a whisper, pointing across the table at the bald-headed man. 'We could tell him . . .'

But before they *could* tell him, the remaining red lights went out and the show started.

As Edinburgh Castle and its esplanade sprang to life on the white table-top in front of them in living, glowing, moving technicolour, Super Gran was scolding herself for being, for once, too slow off the mark. She could easily have opened the door and chased after the thief, *if* she had done it right away instead of hesitating. But he could be anywhere by now. He could have descended the stairs at his leisure and disappeared amongst Edinburgh's tourist hordes.

'Don't worry, Super Gran,' Edison whispered out of the gloom, 'we can tell the man who was robbed that we were witnesses. *And* we can describe the thief, too.'

'Aye, you're right,' Super Gran whispered back. '*Any*one would remember that multicoloured odd-bod.'

Meanwhile the guide, having given his audience a general view of the castle esplanade, operated the Camera's controlling lever, moving the picture on its circular tour of the city immediately below them.

But suddenly, as the picture started to move, Edison shouted: 'Look! There he is! *That's* the one!'

Super Gran and Willard (and the others!) looked where Edison was stabbing her finger excitedly at the table-top – accompanied by 'Quiet!' and 'Shhhh!' from the other viewers. And there he was. The pickpocket.

And he was at it again, near the entrance to the Outlook Tower, just outside the castle esplanade.

The audience, annoyed by all these interruptions from Super Gran and company, were tut-tutting all over the place, in English, Scottish, German, Italian and American!

And the guide, hoping to silence them, succeeded in moving the picture away towards the Grassmarket, at the start of the ten-minute programme.

'No! Wait! Don't move it!' Super Gran called out. 'That's him . . .' The possibility of catching a thief was enough to put the Inventor and his gang out of *all* their minds for the time being. So the Inventor – and the reason for their being there in the first place – forgotten, the trio were more concerned for the moment with being detectives.

Edison startled the bald-headed man by leaning across the table towards him and blurting out excitedly: 'That's the one! He picked your pocket!'

'A couple of minutes ago . . .' Willard added.

'Eh?' the man said stupidly, putting his hand into his pocket. 'What're you talking about?'

'Can't you put the picture back where it was?' Super Gran shouted. 'Near the castle. You'll see him. He's still at it!'

'Hey! Look out, sonny!' the guide muttered, as Willard jostled his arm, trying to make him move the picture back to the esplanade.

'Never mind that, Super Gran.' Edison tugged at her sleeve. 'Why don't you just go after him?'

'Aye!' Super Gran accepted the challenge. 'He's only down at the foot of the Tower, after all.' She dived to the door. 'Let's go!'

She yanked it open and then, closely followed by Willard – and not so closely followed by Edison! – she jumped down the steps to the waiting-room, ran across it through the crowd gathering for the next performance, reached the stairs – and plunged down them, three at a time!

She reached street-level and looked towards the castle. Where was he? Had he escaped? Was she too late? Had she lost him again?

She spotted the man on the castle esplanade, and he was still at it. In broad daylight, in a crowd of sightseers.

'Hey!' she yelled. 'You! You wee scunnery-lugs! Stop! Thief!'

Now usually it's only people in stories, films and comics who shout, 'Stop! Thief!' – but here was Super Gran, in real life, shouting it!

The pickpocket turned, saw Super Gran and melted quietly into the crowd of sightseers milling about the esplanade.

The old lady pointed to his latest victim and yelled: 'Look out! He's picked your pocket! Stop him!'

As she pushed her way through the crowd to reach the thief, she saw out of the corner of her eye the victim taking something *out* of his pocket, looking at it – and smiling.

Smiling? He *shouldn't* have been smiling!

'It's all right,' the man grinned. 'Don't panic.'

The thief hadn't been taking something *out* of the victim's pocket, he had been putting something *in*! And the victim was smiling! Therefore Super Gran jumped to the conclusion that the thief and the victim were in league with one another. The 'victim' must be a spy or a smuggler and the 'thief' was in fact passing on secret plans, diamonds or drugs.

Unfortunately Super Gran, hot on the trail of the pickpocket as he pushed his way through the crowd, didn't stop to wonder why the man was planting things on all sorts of different people. Surely they couldn't *all* be in league with him? Not *all* of them?

She plunged into the crowd after the thief, chasing him across the expanse of esplanade.

After running about a hundred metres towards the castle, with Super Gran gaining on him all the time, the thief turned and looked back at her. He was panting and gasping, like an exhausted Edison. He had a stitch in his side. He stopped. He put one hand out towards the little old lady. To stop her – in case she got hurt!

As if a mere hand could stop a charging Super Gran! It might as well have tried to stop a herd of charging buffalo . . . !

But Super Gran didn't want merely to apprehend the criminal and hand him over to the police. That was too tame. There was no drama – and no fun! – in that. So to liven things up a bit, to make it more interesting for the astonished, staring tourists (who, after all didn't see Super Gran in action *every* day of the week!)

140

she launched herself at the man in a flying rugby tackle.

She caught him round the knees as he turned to run away again and they both tumbled to the ground. As he fell, Super Gran saw the surprised look on his face.

'Aye! You didn't expect that, did you? You wee bachle, you!'

And then, as the odd-bod pickpocket bit the dust, he shrieked – in a very high-pitched soprano voice! And it was then that Super Gran suddenly realized that the odd-bod was more odd than she had thought!

For his cap, wig, beard and eyebrows fell off in the struggle, to reveal – a girl . . . !

14   Castle Capers

'What the . . .? What the heck are you playing at?' the girl mumbled from underneath the untidy heap on the ground. 'What's a . . . little old lady like you . . . attacking a girl for?' She struggled, gasping, to free herself from Super Gran's clutches. 'Come to think of it . . . what's a little old lady . . . attacking *any*one for?'

Super Gran disentangled herself from the girl. 'But – a girl? You're a girl . . .?' She couldn't get over it!

'What did you think I was?' the girl asked as she twisted round to reach her hand into her pocket.

'I thought you were a . . . a . . . a . . .'

PICK POCKET . . .

Super Gran wasn't saying it – she was *reading* it. From a theatre playbill which the girl had pulled from her pocket and was thrusting under the old lady's nose.

Super Gran sprang to her feet like a three-year-old but the girl, not being Super Gran, took a little longer getting there.

As the girl brushed herself down Super Gran picked up her wig, eyebrows, beard and cap and handed them over. 'I thought you were a thief, a spy or a smuggler.'

'Well I'm not. I'm an actress, trying to drum up business for our play *Pick Pocket*.'

Willard and Edison pushed their way through the interested – but puzzled – crowd surrounding Super Gran and the girl, to join them.

'When my "victims",' the girl explained, 'find that someone's slipped playbills into their pockets they'll be so intrigued they'll come and see the play.' She re-fastened her eyebrows, then her beard and wig. 'At least, that *was* the idea.'

'Humph!' Super Gran snorted. 'That's a daft-like idea!'

'Well it wasn't until *you* came along!' the girl retorted – as she straightened her beard!

'But why those colours?' Super Gran asked.

The girl shrugged. 'I'm just a colourful character, I suppose!'

'So it *wasn't* a pickpocket after all?' Edison murmured as they walked away, leaving the actress in a circle of sightseers, putting the finishing touches to her colourful disguise.

'Och well, lassie, how was *I* to know? I did it for the best. And besides, it keeps me in practice, doesn't it?' They headed, automatically, towards the castle. 'And I fairly enjoyed that wee chase and the tackle. Pity she didn't put up more of a fight, isn't it . . . ?'

'Oh, so it's a fight you want, is it?' a familiar voice interrupted. 'Well, I've got the very thing for you . . . !'

They swung round – and came face to face with the Inventor, clutching the Shield, and Rough, Tough and Benny, clutching ropes!

In their excitement Super Gran and company had

forgotten about the Inventor and his mob. But the Inventor and his mob hadn't forgotten about *them*!

They had made their way from the Gardens to the castle, on the chance that Super Gran had headed in that direction. And Gruff, who had been sent to fetch the van, had just arrived with it. He parked it on the esplanade, a few metres away, then jumped out and approached them, making one more Toughie for Super Gran to face!

She looked all round for a way to escape. For, once again, there was no chance of her defeating the Inventor and four Toughies – *plus* the Shield.

'Don't bother looking,' the Inventor gloated. 'There's no escape. You're trapped. And your powers are no use against this!' He held the Shield out towards her and turned, slightly, to his gang. 'Come on boys, line up . . .'

The Toughies took up positions on each side of the Inventor and to his rear, so that they formed a V-shape with the Shield at the point of the V.

Meanwhile, Super Gran and the children had been edging their way backwards, away from the Inventor's mob. But they had now reached the metre-high wall which bordered the dry, grassy ditch in front of the castle. And the drop on the other side of this low wall was about twelve metres! So there was no escape that way either! They were cornered!

Relentlessly the Inventor edged forward towards them, his men, in their V-formation, grinning, their ropes poised, ready to pounce.

'You *know* you can't win this time,' the Inventor sneered.

'But ... but what do you want *Super Gran* for?' Edison asked him. 'You've already *got* Dad's Shield. What more do you want?'

'I want her as a hostage, to make your father work for me. To make me more Shields. To build another Super-machine, to make me a Super-army ...' – his voice rose in a crescendo – '... to rule the world!'

'You're not *still* on about that?' Super Gran murmured. 'You're an awful wee bore of a man! And you're a silly wee haggis-heid and a rotten wee scunner and a ...'

Edison turned to Willard to ask: 'What *is* a "scunner"?'

'*I* dunno!' the boy shrugged.

'And I'm going to make *you*,' the Inventor continued, after the interruptions, addressing Super Gran, 'non-Super again!'

The old lady shuddered at the thought. She couldn't bear being non-Super again. It would mean going back to rheumatics, bad eyesight, a hearing-aid and a walking-stick.

The Inventor moved the Shield forward until it touched Super Gran's chest. 'That's enough of the chatter.' He addressed his gang: 'Right, lads? I'll thump her ...' He held the Shield awkwardly with one hand, to free the other for thumping. 'And you all grab her while she's dizzy. And you,' he nodded to Gruff, 'be ready to drive off the minute the boys get her into the van. Right?'

'Ugh!' replied the talkative Gruff.

'*Do* somethin', Gran!' Willard whispered desperately.

'She can't!' the Inventor snapped. 'She's helpless. And powerless, at last. Or soon will be!'

'Whistle, Super Gran!' Edison whispered, clapping her hands to her ears and nudging Willard to do the same.

This could be their only hope, Super Gran thought, as she pursed her lips and blew.

But nothing happened. At least, not to the Inventor and his mob behind the Shield. To everyone else, yes! Everyone within earshot shuddered and clapped their hands to their ears. But not the baddies. The Super-sound couldn't penetrate the Shield.

'Ha! It didn't work *that* time!' the Inventor mocked.

Super Gran took a deep breath and tried again. And this time the Shield's unbreakable plastic surface creaked and groaned as if the Super-sound was affecting it. The tiny scratches which the surface had suffered, as a result of the wheelchair 'wheelies', opened out slightly into little hair-line cracks.

And, since the Shield couldn't block Super Gran's powers from the rear, she was aware, and had been for the last few minutes, of a sound coming from the castle behind her. And it was music to her ears – but not to the ears of those who don't like the bagpipes! To them it's just a noise – which annoys!

But the sound of the pipes made Super Gran's heart beat faster and the blood pound in her veins, and it gave her courage to face her enemies!

The sound had been increasing in volume as a regimental pipe band marched from the castle parade ground down to the gateway. The others were now also aware of the band, as it emerged through the gateway and crossed the wooden drawbridge on to the esplanade to march past them. Super Gran, Willard, Edison (her hands over her ears!), Benny and the Toughies all turned their heads to watch it pass by. But the Inventor didn't. He, taking no chances, kept his eyes firmly on Super Gran.

'Never mind that!' he snapped. 'You can see a pipe band any time!'

'Especially in Edinburgh,' Super Gran smiled. 'You can't *move* sometimes for pipe bands in Edinburgh!'

'I was just,' the Inventor reminded his gang, 'about to clobber this ... this ...'

'Poor, defenceless, little old lady?' Super Gran suggested, with a wry smile. She might as well end her Super-days with quips on her lips!

'Ready?' The Inventor drew back his fist to clobber her.

Benny got ready to grab her.

Rough and Tough got ready to tie her up.

Gruff got ready to dive towards the van.

Super Gran braced herself.

Edison clung to Super Gran's arm.

Willard closed his eyes.

The pipe band marched past them.

The one o'clock gun boomed out.

The Shield shattered and fell to pieces.

The Shield shattered ...? And fell to pieces ...?

Super Gran, keeping her wits about her, leapt forward. She banged Rough and Tough's heads together. They collapsed in a heap at her feet. She karate-chopped Benny, who collapsed as if pole-axed at the Inventor's feet. She grabbed Gruff, hoisted him over her head, whirled on her toes, put him into an 'aeroplane spin' and released him to land, with a thud and an 'Ugh!', on Rough and Tough as they tried to crawl away! And then she went after their bad boss, who had run off.

The crowd milling about the esplanade stared, fascinated, at the spectacle of a little old lady wreaking havoc on everyone in sight! And they blocked the way of the escaping Inventor who had to veer to the left to dodge them. He looked back over his shoulder at the pursuing Super Gran as he ran blindly towards the pipe band.

'I'll get you, you wee scunnery bachle!' she cried, as she launched herself at him in a flying tackle – her second in ten minutes! The two of them shot forward, embracing each other like goal-scoring footballers – right into the middle of the band!

Bagpipes screeched to a hasty halt, wailing their protests as their players were felled in all directions. Pipers collided with each other and got caught up in the drones, cords, tassels and chanters of each other's pipes. A side-drummer skidded into a tenor-drummer, who skidded into the bass-drummer, whose drum-sticks bopped a piper on the nose. A drum-roll became a drum roll, as a drum rolled away! The drum-major's mace, tossed high in the air at the start of Super Gran's attack, descended – and clobbered two drummers and three pipers!

It was a complete shambles. And the crowd, thinking that it had all been done for *their* benefit, cheered, clapped and yelled for more!

Once the dust had settled, once the last grace-note had faded from the dying, deflated bagpipes, once the last tara-diddle had skittered feebly off the last upright side-drum, once the last army-booted piper had slithered over the esplanade's surface to rest in the heap that had recently been the musical pride of the regiment – Super Gran, in the middle of the heap, looked round. Which was rather difficult – as her head was stuck through the big bass drum!

'Where is he?' she demanded. 'Where's that wee scunnery-heid?'

The Inventor scrambled to his feet, out from underneath the fourteen-stone pipe-major, and started to run limping away. The pipe-major's bagpipes were strung round the Inventor's neck and the chanter squeaked out a note each time the Inventor took a step, for his arm kept accidentally squeezing the bag!

By the time Super Gran had pulled herself out of the heap of mangled military musicians – and her head out of the big bass drum! – Willard and Edison had joined her. But the Toughies had meanwhile recovered and fled. They had staggered, battered, bruised and bewildered, to the stolen van, collecting the Inventor on the way.

*

'But what caused the Shield to shatter?' asked a disappointed but relieved Mr Black that evening, over their meal. He was disappointed by the failure of his latest invention, but relieved that Super Gran and the children had escaped the Inventor's clutches.

'I think it was sound waves that did it,' Super Gran explained. 'It could stand up to all my punches and kicks, but I think some sounds must've been too much for it.'

'The bagpipes, was that it, Gran?' Willard asked. 'Did *they* shatter the Shield?'

An indignant look appeared on his Gran's face, but before she could reply Edison chipped in with:

'Yes! That's what it was! And *I* know how the poor old Shield must have felt! Pipe bands shatter me, too!'

'Tut! Shame on you, lassie,' Super Gran muttered, insulted by her Sassenach friends' nasty comments about her beloved bagpipes.

'So you think acoustics did it, Super Gran?' Mr Black said.

'Acoustics?' The old lady was about to make a Scottish-type joke about 'parasites on a Scots cow' – 'a coo's ticks'! – but she realized that her Sassenach friends might not understand it!

Instead, she said: 'It was either the gun or a combination of the gun *and* the pipes. But don't forget my Super-whistle, that's what started it all. That's what cracked the Shield to begin with, then the gun and the pipes must have finished it off.'

'The gun?' Mr Black looked blank. 'What gun?'

'Oh, you mean the one o'clock gun?' Edison said.

'Yeah,' Willard confirmed. 'I heard a loud bang just before you started attackin' those Toughies, Gran.'

'With the Shield shattered,' Mr Black sighed mournfully, 'I *still* haven't got anything to show to the conference. And it finishes tomorrow.'

'Tell you what,' Super Gran grinned. '*I'll* come along and demonstrate my Super-powers. And you can tell them it was your machine that made me Super in the first place.'

'Well ... all right. That's better than nothing,' Mr Black agreed.

'Huh! You just want to show off again, don't you, Super Gran?' Edison teased.

Her old friend grinned hugely. 'Sure, lassie. Why not?'

Willard frowned, a spoonful of trifle half-way to his eager mouth. 'It's a pity the Inventor and his mob escaped, isn't it? I suppose they'll be on their way back to Chisleton by now.'

But Willard was wrong. They were *not* on their way back to Chisleton. Not just yet, anyway.

A few miles outside Edinburgh they were stopped by the police, who examined their van. A sergeant prowled round it, tut-tutting all over the place, while half a dozen large constables hovered over the Toughies, daring them to sneeze, let alone make a false move!

But the Toughies had no intention of making any moves, false or otherwise. They stood around looking glum, while the Inventor gave them a ticking off.

'Trust you lot! You bunch of morons!' he raged. 'I asked you ... er ... *hinted* at you to "borrow" a van, didn't I? And I asked you ... er ... *hinted* at you to "borrow" one, *this time*, which *didn't* have bald tyres, which *had* a road tax disc and which *didn't* have a number plate missing. And what did you get, eh? What did you get?'

'But this ... van *ain't* ... breakin' the ... law, like,' Benny pointed out, reasonably.

'No! This one *ain't* ... I mean, *isn't* breaking the law,' the Inventor agreed. 'This one *is* the law!'

For the van which the Toughies had stolen *this* time was one that belonged to the Edinburgh police force!

Also by Forrest Wilson

SUPER GRAN

Super Gran Smith hurled herself at young Willard's football in a sliding tackle. 'Come on, laddie, give us a wee kick at your ball!' she cried. Willard stared, amazed, for only a moment ago she had been just an ordinary little old lady sitting on a park bench. But then a beam of blue light shot through her, which was the start of Super Gran, with incredible strength, fantastic speed and X-ray eyes. But Edison knew that Gran's powers had come from a machine invented by her father, and now stolen by the unscrupulous Inventor. So Gran gathers a force of Super-Oldies and goes forward to battle with the Inventor and his Super-Toughies.

SUPER GRAN RULES OK!

Protecting Mr Black's new top-secret invention, the Skimmer, is obviously a job for Super Gran. But when she has to take it to London, all her Super-powers are required to fight off a gang of crooks planning one last job ... not to mention the government's Department Y, who suddenly become Super-interested in the machine!

SUPER GRAN IS MAGIC

Super Gran is touring Britain's top seaside resorts with a new hypnotizing machine that has been invented by Mr Black. Unfortunately, there's a crummy magic act (Mystico and his assistant) also on tour, and they see the benefits of having the machine themselves. So once again, Super Gran has to watch out as the forces of evil close in on her ...

Some other Puffins

FANNY AND THE MONSTERS
Penelope Lively

Filled with a burning ambition to be a palaentologist, Fanny had wickedly slipped away from Aunt Caroline's tour of the Crystal Palace to follow an enticing notice, which read: TO THE PREHISTORIC MONSTERS – not pausing to think about the trouble there would be when her disappearance was noticed . . .

Fanny was always getting into trouble of one sort or another. Being the eldest of a large family was bad enough, but being a girl was worse! There were so many exciting and fascinating things to do, none of which were thought suitable for a young lady in Victorian England. Life, thought Fanny, was very unfair.

I'M TRYING TO TELL YOU
Bernard Ashley

If you had a chance to talk about your school, what would you say . . . honestly? Nerissa, Ray, Lyn and Prakash are all in the same class at Saffin Street School but each of them has something different to say and a different story to tell – all with a real sense of humour that will particularly appeal to readers of about 10.

THE BUNCH FROM BANANAS
David Pownall

The steamy coastal town of Santa Margarita del Banana is notable for two things: its bananas, which are world-famous because they curve the other way, and for Bernard the Boy Detective.

The people in Santa Margarita del Banana are a pretty weird bunch: not just Bernard, but Diablo Dick, the most unsuccessful bandit in history, ex-sleuth Big Fat Joe, the stupidest boy in school, Little Jim Winze, the town barber Hairy von Rijn, and many others. But at least there's plenty to laugh at when the bunch from Bananas is around.

THE MAGIC GRANDFATHER
Jay Williams

Sam had walked in on his grandfather without knocking and surprised him in the middle of practising magic. Not ordinary magic, with tricks and sleight of hand, but *real* magic. Then something awful happened: distracted by Sam in the middle of a complicated spell, Grandpa disappeared – snatched accidentally into another universe. Sam was terrified. How could he explain what had happened to his grandfather? Who would believe him? Most of all, could Sam get his grandfather back? And then he realized that the family talent for magic wasn't as dead as his grandfather had thought...

THE FOX BUSTERS
Dick King-Smith

Ransome, Simms and Jefferies were the three astonishing chickens who were to become a legend to future generations at Foxearth Farm. Not only could they fly out of the reach of foxes, but they found a way of defeating even the most crafty of attacks. Their deeds would be told in years to come by every hen to every brood of chicks, and by every vixen to every litter of foxcubs. For these three sisters were the Fox Busters. A highly original and very funny tale for readers of 8 to 12.

The Bagthorpe Saga
ORDINARY JACK
ABSOLUTE ZERO
BAGTHORPES UNLIMITED
BAGTHORPES v. THE WORLD
Helen Cresswell

A thick but lovable dog who becomes a star, a competition-crazy family, the horrors of Grandma's Family Reunion – these are just some of the hilarious things that happen to the entertaining, eccentric and exasperating Bagthorpe family! Recently featured on television.

Heard about the Puffin Club?

... it's a way of finding out more about Puffin books and authors, of winning prizes (in competitions), sharing jokes, a secret code, and perhaps seeing your name in print! When you join you get a copy of our magazine, *Puffin Post*, sent to you four times a year, a badge and a membership book.

For details of subscription and an application form, send a stamped addressed envelope to:

The Puffin Club Dept A
Penguin Books Limited
Bath Road
Harmondsworth
Middlesex UB7 ODA

and if you live in Australia, please write to:

The Australian Puffin Club
Penguin Books Australia Limited
P.O. Box 257
Ringwood
Victoria 3134